Christmas in Cripple Creek

CRIPPLE CREEK, BOOK 2

SARA R. TURNQUIST

MOUNTAIN
SUMMIT PRESS

If you would like to stay up-to-date on this and other series from Sara and receive a free ebook, sign up for her newsletter:

https://saraturnquist.com/list

CHAPTER 1

Yuletide Preparations

K atherine Sullivan had never been so pleased with herself. She stepped back and looked at the large tree, breathing in the scent of fresh-cut evergreen. Standing tall and proud in the center of Cripple Creek's main street, the tree was a testament to the merriment of the season.

Christmas was upon them with all its wonder and delight. It happened to be Katherine's favorite time of the year. Memories of brown, wrapped packages and peppermint candies flooded her mind. Her skin fairly tingled. Or could it be that she needed to pull her wrap more tightly around herself?

She did so, but it didn't take away the thrill that shot through her. Times spent around each tree placed in this very spot became tangible—with carols and hymns sung by the whole town as they surrounded the fir branches and ribbons with lit candles in hand.

And this year, she bore the responsibility of ensuring the town decorations were just so. How did she land herself in such a position? True, the mayor and his wife were off visiting their eldest for the next few weeks. But was she the best choice for the job?

"Mama!" A little flash of red ran straight for her legs.

Katherine turned as the small girl collided with her skirt. "Susie, be careful." She kept her tone soft, but firm.

The small girl looked up, a smile on her face. "For baby?"

Placing a hand on her rounded stomach, Katherine nodded. "Yes, love, for baby. We have to take care of baby."

Susie flashed her teeth. How could she scold that cute face? It was impossible.

Leaning over, she put a hand on the child's cheek. "I think we need something from the General Store, hmm?"

There was no pretense between them. While Katherine's purpose included checking on the red ribbon in stock, these visits always ended with a sugarcoated something in Susie's hands.

Susie's smile became wider. As did her eyes.

"Yes, please." Her blond curls bounced.

Katherine reached for her hand, and together they walked down the wide dirt-packed road toward the wooden planked sidewalk around the stores.

Breathing in the chilled air, Katherine's oversensitive nose alerted her that Mrs. Abby's café had stew roasting. Her stomach grumbled. Perhaps when Wyatt returned from his house calls, that could be lunch.

Maybe until then she would have to sneak some of that candy promised to Susie.

As they neared the boardwalk, a familiar vibration shook her knees. The thundering of hoof beats shot alarm through her. She jerked her head left and right. Where did it come from?

A cart rushed down Main Street, careening on its way. The driver pushed the horse to move more quickly. Did he not see her and Susie in the road?

The man flung indistinguishable words in her direction. Only she could not work them out.

Susie!

Katherine grabbed for the toddler. She pushed her legs to work faster than they ever had.

The out-of-control horse bore down upon them. Katherine leaped toward safety. She pushed her arms forward, shoving Susie as far out of the way as possible.

Hands gripped Katherine, swinging her farther from danger.

She blinked as the cart passed, pressing Susie's face to her chest.

Who had pulled her to safety? The arms still held her.

She peered up; the man's hands were only then letting go of her arms.

"You all right, ma'am?" The dark-skinned man tipped his hat up, giving her an excellent view of his amber eyes and concerned features.

"Yes, sir. I-I thank you. If you hadn't reached out and..." Tears pricked her eyes. These cursed mood swings!

"Don't you worry none about it. Just glad I could help." The man jerked the brim of his hat downward.

She turned back toward the cart. Where had it stopped? It sat just outside Wyatt's clinic. Why?

A deep voice spoke beside her again. "If you're sure you don't need anything, I best be finding my wife."

She looked at the man who had rescued her and her daughter as she wiped at her eyes. "Of course. Thank you again, Mister..."

"Jeffries, ma'am. Mr. Jeffries."

His deep voice soothed her frazzled nerves.

Katherine nodded. "Mr. Jeffries."

With another nod, he stepped off into the crowd, which parted around him.

She frowned.

In seconds, there was another tug on her arm. "Katie! That was terrifying!"

She knew the voice before she turned. Her brother's wife, Mary. Setting a hand to the one on her arm, she patted it. Though she wanted to throw herself into Mary's arms, she needed to contain her emotion now. That was best. For Susie and for these many onlookers.

"Yes, but all is well now, is it not?" Her words and hands may be shaky, but her features were set.

Mary's eyes widened. "But you can't imagine how afraid I...why I was certain you would be run over."

Katherine rubbed her sister-in-law's fingers as she attempted to look to the happenings at the clinic. "We can't think of what might have been. All we can do, is be thankful for what is."

Mary nodded. "I suppose..." Her voice trailed as her eyes followed where Katherine's gaze landed.

As they watched, the driver knocked on the clinic door.

Nothing.

"Where is Doc?" Mary seemed confused. Why wouldn't Wyatt answer?

Then Katherine remembered—Wyatt wasn't there. He was out on house calls. Katherine must tell this gentleman.

The thought of addressing the man who nearly trampled her made her stomach flip. But there might be an injury. An emergency. Could she find someone to attend to it until Wyatt returned? Perhaps someone should ride after Wyatt?

She pushed forward, handing Susie off to Mary's capable care, and moved toward the clinic.

"Excuse me, sir," she called as she approached, her voice hitching only slightly.

The man turned, his features displaying his urgency. "Where is the doctor, Mrs...."

"Sullivan." She pressed a hand to her chest. "I'm the doctor's wife. He is out visiting his home-bound patients."

"What am I supposed to do with this here fella?" The cart's owner moved toward the back. "I found him out on the trail all busted up. He's in a bad way."

Dare she peer into the cart? She wasn't one of those doctor's wives that could stomach any manner of injury. But she swallowed hard and stepped up to the wagon's bed.

No!

It couldn't be!

Her hand flew to her mouth. She let out a muffled cry.

Flinging a hand to rest on the driver's arm kept her upright.

"What is it, Mrs. Sullivan?"

The world spun.

"S-send for the doctor in Victor."

"What?"

"Just do it!" she screamed.

The man ran off.

She prayed he would make haste.

Clinging now to the side of the wagon, she reached in, fingers grazing the unconscious face of her husband.

"Wyatt..." she cried. "Not now."

What was this darkness that pained him? All Wyatt knew was pain. From everywhere. But he became vaguely aware of hands. Working on him. These hands brought even sharper pain.

Where was Katherine? Was she safe? The children?

What had happened to him?

Everything seemed hazy.

But the hands...they begged him to return to awareness, calling him upward and upward...toward brightness.

Dare he follow? Would the pain become too great?

Would Katie be there? If so, he could manage. Yes, for her, he would chance it.

Pushing his mind to clarity, he forced himself to focus. And open his eyes.

Light overwhelmed him. All that existed was light. Was this heaven?

No, there wouldn't be so much pain.

The darkness invited him back, tempting him to fall into the peace and warmth of its depths.

But there would be no hope of Katie there. And she needed him. He would press on.

Continuing to blink and focus, he turned his head.

A voice cut into the haziness. What did it say?

"...don't...move..."

Don't move? But he must. He would lose this fight if he remained still.

Working through the thick cotton-like confusion, he flexed his fingers.

The presence hovered above him now. And the voice grew louder, more insistent.

But he could make no sense of the words.

Was this friend or foe?

He concentrated. Such a difficult thing.

What was his last memory?

Searching, reaching, he clung to the thin threads of awareness. And he remembered.

His final home visit...Mrs. Shelton...that seemed clearer. It had been routine. But his ride to town...

What happened?

A sound pulsed through him. He'd heard a sound. It had concerned him. Why?

He pushed Rusty faster. But something struck his leg.

The beginning of pain.

Rusty spooked.

The beginning of the end.

Bucking and rearing, the horse would not calm.

Wyatt had been thrown. But he couldn't roll away...his leg had been so heavy...too heavy.

Had Rusty kicked him? Would he be alive if the horse had?

Perhaps he should heed the dark. Let it pull him in.

Katie's face appeared before him. She called to him. Yes, she *did* need him. And their child. Their children. He couldn't give up.

Fighting with everything in him, he pressed up from the surface beneath.

The presence spoke in a harsh tone. Firm hands gripped him. And a cloth covered his nose and mouth.

Chloroform?

No!

He held his breath.

But he knew it was no use. He would either pass out from lack of air or breathe from need. Then he would take in the medicine.

Arms, work. Push it away.

But they couldn't hold him up and push at the presence. How could he do both? There was a way...but he couldn't make it work out in his mind.

He gasped. Only a small breath. Maybe he wouldn't take in too much medicine. But his body cried out for more air. There was no more fighting it. As he breathed in the chloroform, his body succumbed to its effects. Dark tendrils pulled him down...down...down.

Why?

Katherine watched the clinic door, unblinking. Her heart thundered. It would not slow. Not even as the minutes morphed into hours.

What would come of this? Would Wyatt be all right? The depth of sorrow she touched at this thought overwhelmed her. She pulled back from it.

Wyatt *would* be well. He *had* to be.

The door opened.

Dr. Stephen Brown stepped from within the clinic.

Katherine was on her feet the moment the door shifted. She was upon Dr. Brown before she could stop herself. Her hands clutched to her chest, fingers aching at the fierceness of her grip.

"How is he?" She bit at her lip. Would that keep the tears at bay?

Dr. Brown took a step back.

Had she invaded his space? Did she care?

"Dr. Sullivan is out of surgery." He met her gaze, his eyes a cinnamon barrier to his true thoughts. "There was a massive amount of injury from the shotgun blast. But I removed all the pellets."

She took in the information. An arm fell across her shoulders. Turning, she found Pa beside her. He had been so strong for her these last few hours.

"I did what I could to repair the damage. But only time will tell."

Why did he seem discouraged?

"The best thing now is to keep infection from setting in."

She furrowed her brows. Was that likely? Or another one of those things doctors always concerned themselves with? "But will he be all right?"

"He is out of danger," Dr. Brown said matter-of-factly; the

corners of his lips twitched, but did not rise. "However, even after this recovery, he will need to stay off that leg for some weeks."

"Stay off the leg?"

"He could possibly use a crutch to help get around, but he won't be able to stand for any length of time, or put weight on it."

"But he will be fine after, yes?"

Dr. Brown nodded. "Lord willing, he'll come out with a slight limp."

Hugging her father, Katherine didn't bother to hold back fresh tears. Wyatt survived! And he would be well again!

After some moments of giving herself to her emotions, she turned back to Dr. Brown. "May I see him?"

"He is...resting." The doctor's features were stern. "I'd prefer he have time to do so."

Her face fell. She ached to be with her husband. Even if it was just to look at his chest rise and fall from across the room. "W-when can I see him?"

"Perhaps later today." Dr. Brown's eyes were hard. But when he met Katherine's gaze, they softened. "I may take my patient's well-being a bit seriously, but I am not heartless. I understand your eagerness to be with your husband."

Did he? She quieted the protest that almost escaped her lips. And nodded.

"I will send for you at the earliest possible moment."

Swallowing, she searched out Pa's hand. She slipped her hand into his and held fast to it.

Pa let out a breath through his teeth. Had she gripped him so hard?

"Please do so, doctor." Pa's words were firm.

Dr. Brown nodded and backed into the clinic, shutting the door behind himself.

"How can he do this?" Katherine turned to those who had assembled in wait with her—Pa, David, and Mary.

"It's for the best," her brother said, laying a hand on her shoulder. "You know Wyatt would do the same."

She did know, but she didn't have to like it. What was she supposed to do for...who knew?...perhaps hours...until Dr. Brown declared it safe for her to be with Wyatt?

Mary stepped closer. "Let's get you something to eat." She looped an arm through Katherine's. "I don't think you've eaten a thing. And that baby needs you to."

Katherine opened her mouth to argue, but at the very mention of the baby, her prepared argument fell flat. She would do anything for this baby...Wyatt's baby.

Nodding, she allowed Mary to lead her toward the café.

The two men took up step behind. They conversed, but in such low tones that Katherine couldn't make out anything said. Or perhaps she was too absorbed in her own thoughts.

"You'll feel better about everything after you've had a solid meal," Mary continued. "Food always makes everything better." She let loose a little laugh.

From the woman's lithe figure, one would never guess she held such an opinion. She was slender from every angle.

Not that Katherine's own appetite reflected a hesitancy to eat...especially now. Even when not pregnant, she had a curvier figure than her sister-in-law. All the more so now. But she would not begrudge the extra weight she carried for the baby.

Wyatt certainly didn't.

Her face warmed. She'd best not follow that line of thinking any further. Not when Pa and David were just behind her.

Still, she might as well give herself over to whatever distractions they could offer.

Wyatt opened his eyes. This time, he was not stung by the brightness around him. His surroundings were dimly lit. He attempted to take it in. Where was he?

The familiar accouterments of the recovery room became visible. Though scantly furnished, the simple pieces were a relief to see. And the window's curtains had been drawn, allowing precious little light to enter the space.

He breathed out, thankful the assault on his senses had been thus lessened. Dark and quiet, he found the room more like the darkness he had come from than not.

Except...

His body hurt. In multiple places. The places where he throbbed and ached were many.

Could he sit up? He pressed off the mattress, wanting to straighten his upper body.

That was a mistake.

Those pains sharpened and cried out. Loudly.

He fell back to the bed.

Dare he call for assistance? Who would come? Katherine?

Should he chance it?

As this was one of the recovery rooms in his clinic, chances were good that he was among friends. Perhaps Katie waited downstairs for him to rouse.

He blinked. Though the pain was great, he lived. But who had patched him up? The dentist with a doctor complex? Or had they gone to Victor for the ever stoic Dr. Brown?

He prayed the latter.

Unable to examine his wounds for the manner of care they had been given, he was uncertain.

Maybe he should try once more to sit up.

Inching his arms toward midback didn't prove so difficult.

Then he pressed his hands into the softer surface beneath himself.

His arms shook and faltered.

He could not hold the position.

As he released his muscles, his elbow shot out and knocked the side table. Something fell, shattering on the floor.

Whether he wished it or not, whoever was downstairs would know he had wakened.

He settled himself. Now all there was to do was wait.

Sure enough, footfalls on the stairs soon followed. The stairs squeaked. Those steps were heavier than a woman's. Not Katherine.

His mood dipped. How he wanted to see his beloved wife! For her to know that he was well. For him to know that she was, too.

The door opened a crack. Did someone peer in?

Wyatt glared at the opening; still he could not make anything out in this dimness.

"Who is there?" Wyatt ground out, teeth clenched from frustration as much as pain.

The door swung wider.

"Dr. Brown." The man entered the room, eyes scanning Wyatt's figure. "How are you?"

Wyatt squinted at the silhouette. "Is that you, Stephen?"

As the physician moved closer, his features cleared.

Wyatt grimaced. "Is this more of your handiwork?"

Brown crossed the room and opened the curtains. Light flooded the room.

Wyatt saw his pseudo-friend's face without hindrance. "That's better. Thanks."

Brown grabbed the back of a chair and pulled it closer to the head of the bed before sitting. "You've been through it, Sullivan."

Wyatt held his gaze. "Tell me."

Stephen Brown crossed his arms. "Where do I start? Contusions, abrasions, bruised ribs, probably strained muscles. And shotgun blast to the leg."

Widening his eyes, Wyatt breathed heavier as he lifted his head. Could he see the injury from here? "Shotgun?"

Brown nodded. "Left leg. I removed the pellets, of course, and cleaned up the mess. Mind telling me what you remember?"

He would never be able to see his leg from this angle. Wyatt dropped his head to the pillow as he examined the ceiling. His breath released slower. "I can tell you what I know. I was headed back to town after my last home visit."

Searching, he tried to put the pieces of random strands of memory together in some logical way.

"And?"

"I heard the shotgun fire. It spooked my horse. Then he freaked out. Threw me, kicked me, not sure what else."

Brown put a hand to his chin. "I don't think you'll be walking for some time."

"You don't know me." Wyatt smiled, gaze still on the boards that made up the ceiling.

"But I do know medicine."

Wyatt nodded. That was true. Brown had always been an excellent physician. What he lacked in bedside manner, he made up for in his ability to diagnose.

"Come now, Sullivan. You can't be too proud to use a crutch, can you?"

Wyatt grimaced. A crutch. He was not in favor of it. But could he escape the reality of it? Truth was, he should be thankful to be alive. He very well could have bled out on the trail.

"How'd I get here?"

"Seems a man found you out there—brought you back. That's what I know. I wasn't here. They sent for me after he was gone." Brown quirked a brow. "Your wife bandaged your wound and stopped the bleeding until I could get here."

Katherine? Working on his wound? That didn't seem likely. "Truly? My wife?"

"That's my understanding." Brown shrugged. "She was adamant to assist in surgery, but I refused."

Wyatt nodded. That was best. No need to have her going squeamish during the procedure. Or even fainting. "Where is she?"

"Somewhere in town, I figure. I'll send for her." He stood. "Promised her I would do so as soon as you were awake."

Good old Stephen. Ever the vigilant doctor. But the man had utilized his skills on Wyatt and he would be all the better for it. He couldn't imagine what kind of hack job that dentist would have done.

"You're a good man, Stephen." Wyatt met his gaze. "And an excellent physician. Thank you."

Brown offered him a half-smile. "You'd do the same for me."

Not much for sentiment. Wyatt expected no less.

With that, Brown moved to the door and stepped out. Wyatt was left with his thoughts. And his ever-growing eagerness to see Katherine.

CHAPTER 2

Christmas Secrets

Katherine rushed into the clinic, eyes darting, trying to find any sign of life.

Dr. Brown sat at Wyatt's desk.

"Is it true?" She leaned over the desk. Papers shook under her hands. Was she trembling?

Dr. Brown stared, mouth agape.

Why wouldn't he answer? "Is Wyatt awake?"

"Y-yes, ma'am. He is." Dr. Brown rose. He straightened his jacket and moved toward the stairs.

He needn't bother. She turned and shot off. Nearly halfway to the stairs, Dr. Brown cleared his throat.

"A moment first, please," he called. His voice did not invite discussion.

Loathed to pause, she halted, though everything in her cried out for her to continue.

She took in a breath before she turned. This had best be important.

His gaze caught hers, steely eyes pinning her. "There is something we should discuss."

The sweetest voice whispered over Wyatt. Could it be? Katie?

Had he fallen into sleep once more?

The scent of lilacs came over him, drawing him to her. He breathed in the aroma now associated only with his wife. His lips curved upward. No dream could keep him.

He opened his eyes. And there, sitting on the edge of his bed, was his wife.

Tears filled her eyes.

Had she been crying or were these fresh?

"Wyatt!" She fell onto his chest.

He choked on his breath at the pain, but let no sound escape. He lifted his lame hands and pressed them to her shoulders. "Yes, my love, I'm all right."

She pulled back only enough to look into his eyes. "I thought...when I saw you in the back of that cart...I was so afraid that you..." Sobs overtook her and she nuzzled her head into his neck.

"God had me in His care the entire time," he spoke into her hair. "And we know we can trust Him."

She nodded. But the moisture wetting his collar contradicted her belief. Or were they only the release of her fears?

Leaning up once more, she laid her hand on the side of his face. "What would I do if I lost you?"

Her eyes filled again. She bit at her lip.

Did she need a response? The brief seconds ticked by, adding to one another. As he pushed forth words, she spoke. "I would be undone."

He gripped her forearms. She anchored him more than she knew. "Thankfully, we don't have to find out."

Her eyes, reddened from her emotion, continued to drink him in.

He longed to wipe at the tears, but his limited strength would not permit him to lift his arms so high.

"Are you...?" As the words escaped, she thinned her lips. Did she hold back other concerns? What kinds of reassurances did she need? What could he offer?

"Yes, I am well. I have some bruises and cuts. My leg is the worst of it. But I will heal." He stroked her arms with his thumbs as he continued to hold her there.

She sniffled and nodded.

"Now, let us talk of it no more. I want to hear how you are. And the baby." He threaded a hand between them, resting it on her swollen abdomen.

She pressed her hands over his. "All is well."

There was hesitancy in her voice. Was she hiding something? Would she speak of it?

"But...?" he offered.

Peering down at him, she held his gaze and then looked away. "It is nothing."

Nothing? What was nothing?

She stood and walked to the window.

Why did she have to do that? Move away from him when he could not follow?

"It's not nothing." His voice was firm. He pushed against the mattress, lifting his upper body. The same pains slammed him back. Fighting the urge to swear, he calmed his breathing. "Something is bothering you."

She looked at the floor. Why would she not share what burdened her so?

"Katie?"

Silence.

Gritting teeth, he pressed into the bed again until he reclined. His concern gave him added strength.

"Katie..." he warned, his voice no longer as soft as he wished it to be.

She glanced at him. "I don't wish to upset you. Haven't you been through enough?"

Not want to what? What exactly would be so bothersome? "*This* is upsetting me."

She dropped her hands to her sides and pushed out a breath. Was she now resigned? "All right."

His brows furrowed, but he waited.

"The cart that carried you into town...well, it came in rather...quickly."

Where was this going?

"Susie and I were in the middle of the street."

Dear God, no. His chest tightened.

"It nearly ran us over."

Nearly?

She crossed back toward him. "We're fine. Everyone is fine. I'm fine. Susie is fine. The baby is fine. But—"

"Are you certain?" he challenged.

"Yes." She put hands to her abdomen as if in defense. "I felt the baby move since then. Several times."

The fist closed around his heart did not let up.

"And Susie is unharmed," she continued. "Maybe a little upset, but there is not a scratch on her."

He closed his eyes and dropped his head back. Nearly run over by a horse and cart. And he hadn't been there. What would he have done? Could his heart take so much?

Katie sat on the bed's edge, taking one of his hands in hers.

Wyatt gripped it, bringing his other hand around to sandwich her more delicate one.

"All *is* well." She leaned forward. "As you said—God was looking out for us." A slow smile crept onto her features.

Trusting God with his family was much harder than asking her to trust his life into the hands of their Heavenly Father. Perhaps a lesson he need delve into deeper.

He squeezed her hand and looked for relief to fill her

features. It did not. Was there something else? "What do you hold back?"

She chewed at her lower lip. "I'm uncertain about what Dr. Brown said." Her eyes became serious again, and her smile fell.

"What do you mean?" What could Stephen have said that would bother her? Did she not like the idea of Wyatt relying on a crutch? It would be an adjustment for them all.

"About the delivery."

"What?" Why would Stephen be speaking with her about their baby's delivery?

Katie's eyes clouded. Was she trying to hold back again? Did she think she shared something she shouldn't have? That she burdened him?

He forced his features to remain neutral. "Dr. Brown should not be telling you things that are kept from me. Especially where our baby is concerned."

She drew in a breath. "He said that *he* would be delivering our baby."

Stephen? Delivering Wyatt's baby? Why would he presume so? Did he think Wyatt incapable? Just because of some leg wound? Why wouldn't Wyatt be able to stand for the delivery come that time? Or was it more than that?

Wyatt took in a deep breath. He best not let Katie see how it disturbed him. "Do not worry so with Brown's words. This is only a misunderstanding. *I* will deliver our baby. No one else."

She let out a burst of air. "That makes me feel so much better." Falling forward again, she embraced her husband.

And he, again, held back any sign of the pain that shot through him. But of this he was determined: He *would* be the one delivering his child. And he would have a conversation with Stephen Brown about overstepping.

What could the man be thinking?

Christmas approached. It would not wait. Not for her. Not for Wyatt to recover. Not for anything.

And so, Katherine found herself back in the town square, approving decorations and checking things off her mental list.

She had left Wyatt at home. Would he be well enough to care for himself? He'd made steady improvement this past week. For which she was thankful.

His successes had been nothing short of amazing. It seemed as if he was determined to outdo Dr. Brown's assessment of his recovery time. Yet it had kept her indoors, tending to him, much of these last few days.

Not that she minded. She loved spending this time with him. But she missed getting ample fresh air and stretching her legs.

Still, she worried. Would he overdo it without her there to pace him?

"Well?"

Katherine jerked her attention in the direction of the voice.

Mary stood on the balcony of the boarding house, staging decorations. How long had she been holding the wreath up for Katherine's approval?

"I think it needs to be a couple of inches to the right."

Mary obliged her, moving the green fir circlet as directed.

"Perfect!" What would Katherine do without Mary? She had been irreplaceable during the planning and decorating. How fortuitous that Mary's youngest joined his sister in school. The only toddler underfoot had been Susie, but today she was home with Wyatt.

Another layer to Katherine's anxiety. What if the little girl proved too much for Wyatt?

"I think that's it up here," Mary called.

Katherine nodded, forcing her focus to stay on the present as she waved her friend's descent from the second-floor walkway. "Come on down."

A growl rumbled in Katherine's stomach. Food would become a necessity in short order.

Mary came up alongside her. "Are we almost finished here?"

Katherine's lips widened into a smile. Mary apparently had similar thoughts about lunch. "Shall we see what Mrs. Abby has cooking?"

"I thought you'd never ask!" Mary leaned against Katherine, feigning weakness.

Katherine pushed at her. "Let's go."

Turning toward the café just down the short stretch of boardwalk, Katherine's thoughts shifted. The sheriff had spoken with her this morning, but she was none too pleased with what he had to say.

No hope.

They gave up the manhunt for the shooter. What else could they do? There wasn't even a description. The man who brought Wyatt in had been found and questioned. He hadn't seen the culprit either.

So, it would remain a mystery.

Unless...

She shuddered. *Unless he or she strikes again.*

"You all right?" Mary's gentle voice interrupted.

Katherine shook her head. "Just thinking."

"That's never good."

Shooting a look at Mary, Katherine caught the barely contained smile. She bumped her sister-in-law with her shoulder.

Soon enough, they approached the café. The smell of pot roast wafted from the open doors. Katherine took it in.

Her mouth watered.

Grabbing for her arm, Mary prodded her onward. "I can already taste it!"

It took only moments to get seated at their favorite table by one of the café's windows. From this vantage point, they could watch the goings on in the center of Cripple Creek.

Mrs. Abby stopped by shortly thereafter. She filled their glasses with water. "What'll ya have?"

She had not been quite as cordial with Katherine as she was when Katherine courted Reverend Timothy Johnson. He had always been a favorite of Mrs. Abby's. Still, Katherine was relieved she could once again patronize this establishment without becoming the object of scorn.

"Two pot roast plates, please." Mary smiled at the older woman.

"It'll be out soon, ladies." Mrs. Abby gave each of them a curt nod.

Then again, maybe Katherine did have to endure the simple pleasantries kept...well, simple and to the point.

A voice bellowed from the entrance.

Mr. Yerby came in with Mr. Hammond.

The banker was boisterous as ever. "Yerby, can you imagine? A train! Coming right here to Cripple Creek!"

They took the only table available, next to Katherine and Mary.

Train? Katherine mouthed to Mary.

"How do ya do, Mrs. Sullivan, Mrs. Matthews?" Mr. Yerby paused next to his seat.

Mr. Hammond did the same.

"We are well." Katherine offered the General Store owner a smile. And nodded toward Mr. Hammond.

"How is Doc?" Hammond rumbled. "I do hope he'll be back in the clinic soon."

Katherine's smile wavered. When would Wyatt be able to return to the work he loved so much? "He is home, resting. I think he is more eager than you to take up his practice again.”

Hammond nodded.

Mr. Yerby looked at the women with that twinkle in his eye. “What brings you to town?”

“We are seeing to the town’s Christmas preparations.” Mary spoke up. “Katherine is wearing many hats, as usual.”

“Looks mighty fine. I can’t remember when I saw the boarding house so festive.” Mr. Yerby winked.

“Perhaps Mrs. Sullivan should see to the town’s upcoming preparations.” The banker elbowed Mr. Yerby. “This place could handle some better upkeep.”

More work? And the whole of the town? Katherine opened her mouth to make a polite protest, but was cut off.

“It can’t happen soon enough.” Mr. Yerby pulled his chair back from the table.

Katherine’s brows came together. “Soon enough? For what?”

“Why, the train, dear Mrs. Sullivan!” Mr. Hammond’s eyes widened. Was he so surprised she hadn’t known? “The train!”

“Oh, you remember, Katie,” Mary offered. “The two railroads competing to reach Cripple Creek first?”

That did seem familiar. Had she been so caught up in her own life that she could have forgotten something so important?

“Exactly!” Mr Hammond beamed. “The Florence and Cripple Creek Railway has nearly won.”

“It will change everything.” Mr. Yerby met Katherine’s gaze. “For my business. For your husband’s. And even for Hammond here.”

“I...suppose.” Katherine sipped from her glass. Had she and Wyatt not discussed this?

She searched her memory. There was only a vague recollection of such a conversation. But it didn't seem as if it went so strongly in favor of the train's coming. Yes, Wyatt welcomed the speed at which supplies could come, but he worried about the loss of the life they knew. What else, he had said, might the train bring?

"You'll see. It will mean wonderful things for Cripple Creek!" Mr. Hammond declared.

Mrs. Abby's serving girl stopped at the table with two plates of pot roast. She set one in front of Mary, and the other before Katherine.

"We don't want to disturb your meal," Mr. Yerby said, tipping his hat toward Katherine, then toward Mary. "Tell Doc we all hope he is recovered quickly."

"I will." Katherine smiled.

The two men returned to their banter as they sat. They removed their hats and continued chatting about the importance of the railroad.

All the while, Katherine became more and more uncertain it was the harbinger of good things as they suspected. What if it brought with it more saloons? More gambling? More unseemly behavior?

Because in her experience, when the town boomed, it was *that* sort that caused the population to grow.

Wyatt hobbled toward the steaming pot. There was no other way to put it. That's how he got around. Hobbling...leaning heavily on a crutch. He couldn't function without it. No matter how he tried, how hard he pushed himself...he just couldn't get away from his reliance on it. No two ways about it.

Susie scrambled underfoot.

That didn't help matters.

"Don't make Pa trip." He forced his tone to remain light and easy, though moisture beaded on his forehead.

Not that she could understand his frustration.

She giggled and ran between his legs.

He struggled to maintain his balance. And even so...just barely.

"Susie!" he barked. As soon as the words were out, he wished them back. He hadn't intended to speak so harshly.

Her wide eyes watered and her lip quivered.

Why had he spoken so?

Dragging himself to a nearby dining chair, he sat and bid her come.

She did...with slow, reluctant steps.

It tore at his heart.

As she neared, he scooped her up and set her on his good leg.

"Susie, Pa is not angry. I'm only worried. About your safety. When you run around my legs, I might fall. That would hurt me and could hurt you. You understand?"

She nodded; big tears made trails down her chubby cheeks.

"Pa loves you forever to the moon." He let his smile fill his face before he pressed a kiss to her hair.

How had he gotten himself in this mess? Completely lost to these two ladies—Katherine and then Susie. It wasn't so long ago he was on his own, doing as he pleased, making his way in life, uncaring of others' opinions.

Now this.

But he knew—this was so much better.

Just as much as they had his heart, he had theirs. And Jack's. The boy that grew like the wild grass.

Shouldn't he be home from school by now? Where was he anyway?

Susie patted his cheek. "Pa fuzzy."

He grinned. "Yes, Pa could use a shave."

"I like Pa fuzzy." She giggled. "Like a bear."

"You'd better hide," he said as he set her onto her feet. "This Papa Bear is going to come and get you!" He stood, raised his arms, and growled.

She shrieked and ran off toward the hall.

He grabbed for the table as she disappeared, having leaned a bit too far when he launched himself upward. Had she seen his weakness?

He reached for his crutch. She may have the head start, but he would follow and continue their game. After all, he was well enough.

But as he had stood, the chair had nudged the crutch a bit farther away. Now it sat at a precarious angle against the table. If he didn't capture it with one decisive swipe, it would fall for certain.

He bent from the waist and stretched out his arm.

Not quite enough.

Pushing farther, he put more weight on his good leg and gained some inches. His fingers grazed the crutch.

Just a little more...

No!

It fell in the opposite direction, the wooden implement clattering to the floor.

And he soon after. The chair did nothing to brace his fall, but instead created an obstacle, bruising him and his pride further.

He landed, his arms and legs askance, pain shooting from his leg and his opposite hip where the impact against the chair had been the worst.

But he bit back any sound. He would not scare Susie. Or make known his clumsiness.

The front door shut.

Wyatt closed his eyes. Why must Jack come home to find him thusly? Would his pride ever recover?

"Pa?" Jack called.

Had he spotted Wyatt on the floor? Or did he seek out his father's whereabouts, unaware? Dare Wyatt call to him? Reveal his location? There was little point in delaying Jack's finding him.

"Here I am," he pushed out through gritted teeth.

"Pa!" Jack rushed to him. "What happened?" He scanned the scene. No doubt using some of that deductive reasoning he fancied in that book detective...Sherlock Holmes.

"It's not important." Wyatt kept his voice even. "Please. Just help me up." How humiliating! He needed his eight-year-old son to assist him. Was he truly so helpless?

Jack's eyes moved left to right. Was he still taking it in? "What should I do, Pa?"

Wyatt managed to twist around and look at his son. "If you set the chair upright, I think I can use it to get myself up."

The boy's mouth turned downward on one side. Skeptical? Perhaps rightfully so. The scene must appear impossible.

"Let's just try." He waved Jack toward the chair.

The youngster set the chair in place as told.

Wyatt then set his hands on the seat and worked to pull himself up.

Smaller hands came around his back and sides, jerking him upright as well. Jack?

He mustn't! He might injure himself.

Jerking his head toward the boy, he found he could no more scold the boy's effort than swallow his own pride.

So, little by little, inch by inch, they worked until Wyatt sat in the chair once more. Wyatt's breaths came heavily. As he slowed his own breathing, he heard that Jack, too, worked for air.

"I think that's all the help you should offer." Wyatt set a hand to Jack's arm. "Thank you."

Jack smiled.

He caught and held Jack's gaze for a moment. "Can you find your sister for me? She is hiding in one of the bedrooms."

Jack nodded and went off after his charge.

Wyatt collapsed his upper body onto the table. Why did Jack have to see him like that? Why was he so weak?

But this pity wouldn't do any of them any good. Katie least of all. She had carried such a heavy burden since his injuries. And he would not weigh her further.

He must find a way to replenish his strength—and fast—she was due home any moment.

CHAPTER 3

Will the Merriment Ever End?

K atherine maneuvered the horse and cart to the homestead. It had been quite a day. How would she ever accomplish it all? Preparing the town for the season and coordinating the festivities all while caring for Wyatt, the home, and the children—an overwhelming list.

She slowed the horse and carefully lowered herself from the seat. No easy task with her growing midsection. But soon enough, she stood on solid ground.

Taking in a long breath, she looked at the post in front of the house. How nice it would be to put the horse there, and wait for Wyatt to manage the animal and cart. Or leave it for later. But that would serve no one. Wyatt wasn't in any condition to handle the horse and cart. It was up to her.

She made the shortest work possible of stabling the horse, but she was still sweating by the time she was done. This wasn't how she wanted to greet her husband.

Oh well.

Making her way up the steps and into the house, she wanted to collapse in her armchair or perhaps the bed. She didn't even care about dinner. Still, someone had to provide nourishment for the children and Wyatt.

She shrugged out of her coat and hung it by the door.

"Mama!" That flash of blonde ran straight for her legs, hugging onto her.

She put a hand to Susie's curls. "Hello, sweet girl. How is Mama's angel?"

The girl peered up at her. "Pa fall down."

"What?" Was he well? Injured? Katherine looked around, searching. She spotted Wyatt with Jack by the dinner table, setting out plates. At every seat.

Why so many?

"Fell down?" Katherine murmured, more to herself.

Susie toddled toward the great room, to a collection of blocks and a half-constructed building.

Katherine stepped toward her husband.

He looked up as she approached. A smile crossed his features and he opened his arms in her direction.

She longed for his embrace, despite her concern. His comfort, his warmth, and the surety of his love were all desperately needed.

Walking into his arms, she wrapped hers around his shoulders. And he enfolded her, holding her close.

"How are you?" she whispered.

He leaned back just far enough to catch her eyes.

"Well enough." He tipped her face upward with a finger under her chin. "What about you?"

She grimaced. Would he avoid the issue? "I'm all right. But I'm not worried about me. Susie said you fell."

Wyatt's mouth became a thin line. "I wish she hadn't. It was nothing. A little accident."

Katherine furrowed her eyebrows.

"Truly, my love. A little slip. Nothing more," he insisted,

eyes scanning her features. "I'm more concerned about how tired you look."

She frowned. Forcing the issue would produce nothing but defensive words between them. "Today was rather full."

Reaching up, he moved a strand of hair behind her ear. "Perhaps you should pass this position onto someone else."

She squared her shoulders and met his gaze. "I'm committed now. That wouldn't be right."

He shrugged. "Just a thought."

She bristled. How could he not understand?

He grinned. "I have another thought..."

"Oh?" A smile tugged at the corners of her mouth.

"Oh yes." His fingers caressed the side of her face. "I have been remiss in welcoming my wife home...properly."

She worked to keep a straight face. "That is true."

He moved his face nearer. "That...I intend to remedy."

A murmured response was all she managed as his lips pressed against hers.

All thoughts vanished as she became lost in that world that belonged to her and Wyatt alone. A place where all that existed was this excitement, this stirring in her midsection, spreading like wildfire. And the reality of *him*—his scent, his body, his lips' movement on hers.

When he pulled back again, her head spun. But he didn't release her. And she wondered as always—did he know she was light-headed? Is that why he held onto her? Or because he was?

After some moments passed and she returned to solid ground, she remembered the extra plates on the table.

She pulled back a little more. "Why so many settings for dinner?"

"Oh." He looked at the table as if he, too, were surprised. Then his eyes caught hers again. "I have something I hope will cheer you up..."

Why was she afraid it would do nothing of the sort?

"I invited your parents and your brother's family over for dinner."

Katherine's mouth fell. There were things she wanted to say, and things she best not say.

Wyatt had likely done this for her, truly hoping to give her a surprise gift of some sort. She enjoyed her family. But tonight she was tired...so tired. How could she sit through a large family meal when all she wanted was to lay down and forget dinner altogether? Even more...what would she say to Wyatt at this moment?

Honesty. Always best.

"I...don't know what to say."

He pressed a quick kiss to her forehead. "Don't say anything. The food is almost done."

"You...have dinner ready?" What else had he been up to? Had he pushed himself too far?

"Yeah." He shot her one of his more charming smiles. "I'm not completely useless." Stepping away from her, he disentangled his arms and hobbled toward the oven.

"Wyatt..." What could she say? Did she wish to chastise him? But dare she let him continue to do these things...so much that it compromised his recovery?

She glanced at Jack. He had moved toward the great room and assisted Susie with her block creation. Good. He didn't need to be privy to this interchange.

Wyatt stirred something that smelled divine. The smell of baked chicken carried across the room.

"Wyatt."

He set the spoon down and stared out the window. "Don't say it." His brilliant blue eyes turned on her. "I know you want me to be careful. But I can't sit around and let you do everything. I can't."

How could she express herself without challenging him?

"And I can't watch you wear yourself to the bone." His eyes were serious.

She frowned.

"Especially not now." His gaze shot toward her abdomen.

She took a few steps, closing the distance between them. "What would you say to one of your patients with these same injuries?"

He licked his lips and glanced at the ceiling, letting out a breath.

"I worry about you." She moved closer. They were only an arm's length apart.

His gaze captured hers again. "I understand. And I would be understanding toward a patient with a very pregnant wife."

Katherine quirked a brow and tilted her head. She knew him better than that. "Would you?"

He looked down but peered up at her after a moment. "You have no right to be so familiar, Mrs. Sullivan." Reaching out, he grabbed her and pulled her to himself. "And use it against me."

"I have every right." She laid a hand to the side of his face, feeling the scruff there. Her heart thumped harder. There was no denying she liked this unshaven look. "And you know it."

He claimed her lips once more, a wilder, more passionate kiss.

When they broke, he lay his forehead against hers. "All right. I'll slow down. *If* you will."

She nodded against him. "Deal."

Only time would tell if he would uphold his end of the bargain. Or if she would.

As for now, however, the sound of hoof beats outside alerted them that someone had arrived.

"That was delicious!" Lauren Matthews blotted her lips with her linen napkin.

Wyatt smiled despite himself. Impressing Katherine's mother was always an added bonus.

"I don't know how you manage," Mary added. "In town all day working on the Christmas festivities and then home to create this wonderful spread."

He felt Katherine's eyes on him. Now he wished she wouldn't have to give him credit. If only she would let the comment slide.

But she wouldn't.

"It wasn't me." She coughed into her napkin.

Wyatt's eyes found hers. Dare he betray the sympathy he had for her? Would she read it as pity?

"Wyatt is responsible for this evening's meal."

Tom clapped him on the back. "Well now, Doc. I knew you were a good cook. But you outdid yourself tonight. And hobbling around to boot."

He smiled at his father-in-law, but his gaze soon found Katherine's again.

Her eyes were turned toward the table's surface. And there was no mistaking the rise of color in her cheeks.

"Are you warm, Katie?" her brother asked. Must he?

"Oof!" David muffled a yelp, drawing Wyatt's regard. Mary pulled her elbow back to her side.

"What?" David rubbed his arm.

"It's nothing." Katherine gave David the courtesy of an answer. "I'm just a bit..." But her words trailed off. How could she answer that?

"As you probably remember, David, pregnancy can make a woman flush at a moment's notice," Wyatt offered. Hopefully Katherine would accept his assistance.

The look she shot him did not appear thankful.

He wished he could get up and gather dishes...or disappear...anything to remove himself from this situation.

"Yeah, I remember," David said, glancing at his wife. Still, he didn't seem any more convinced.

An awkward silence fell over the room.

"Let me help with these dishes." Mary stood.

"Me too." Lauren was also on her feet in a moment.

Katherine rose.

Lauren put out an arm. "You've done too much already today, sweetheart. Rest."

"But—" Katherine grabbed her own plate as she turned.

Mary took it from her. "You heard your Ma. You've earned some time off your feet. If not for yourself, for that baby."

Wyatt shuddered inside. The last thing Katherine would appreciate was her family coddling her. His strong, independent wife...made to sit back and watch others clean her kitchen. It couldn't be easy.

He set a hand on hers and gave it a gentle squeeze.

She did not so much as peer in his direction. Was she angry with him? Hurt perhaps?

"So, Doc, I hear the train's coming sooner than expected." Tom took a swig of his drink.

"Most people are expecting it to arrive before spring." David laid his forearms on the table where his plate had been.

"Won't that be something," Wyatt said without thinking much on it. His focus remained on Katie. Was she well? Or had she become overstressed?

"I think it's about time this town made progress." David eyed his father. Something seemed strained in their shared gaze. What was it?

Wyatt pulled his attention from Katie to the conversation.

"Young folks are always talking about 'progress.' But are you careful to count the costs?" Tom raised an eyebrow.

David eased back in his chair, crossing his arms. It became

apparent they'd had this discussion before. Did David expect Wyatt to intervene? Take sides?

"Won't the train bring supplies more quickly?" Katie inserted.

So she intended to speak on this subject? She typically steered clear of family disputes that didn't involve her and Wyatt. The relationship between her father and brother could be...complicated.

"That's what I've been saying to Pa." David waved a hand in Tom's direction. "We wait so long for things. Mr. Yerby has to order what he doesn't have in stock. And then we wait. The train will not only get our orders to us quicker, it will reduce the price. Even I can count *those* costs."

Tom furrowed his brows.

Wyatt's stomach did a little flip. He had been so grateful to become a part of a close-knit family. And one that had less dysfunction than his—a drunken mess of a father who beat his mother and even Wyatt when he'd stepped in to defend her.

To see these two men argue was difficult, but Wyatt could manage it. For in this family, their love ran deep. Too deep for anyone to come to blows.

But David speaking to his father with a disrespectful tone strained Wyatt's patience. Dare he put forth his opinion?

"Surely you see that's not all there is to it." Katie jerked her head to face her brother. "Just as the train brings large amounts of supplies, it will bring an increase of the town's population." Her words were curt.

David's eyes widened a little and his brows raised. "What would be the problem with that? Unless you, like Pa, expect nothing but riffraff."

Katie's eyebrow quirked. "You must consider that with the good comes the...not so good."

Was it Wyatt's imagination or did she tremble? He intertwined their fingers.

At last, she looked at him. Her eyes welled with emotion, but the corners of her lips tipped upward.

They would be all right. He let out a breath.

"I won't hear it." David uncrossed his arms and placed his hands on the edge of the table. "I refuse to live with that kind of pessimistic outlook on mankind, on God's plan. Make no mistake, the train *is* coming. And all we can do is try to make the best of it. I, for one, choose to trust that God will prosper us *and* our town."

David's words made sense. The time to decide if the railroad would come had passed. There was little sense in discussing views on that now. It was up to God and His plan as to the outcome.

Standing, David nodded. "If you'll excuse me, I promised Jessie and Peter I'd make something with them tonight. Y'all do have the best blocks in Cripple Creek."

That drew a smile out of Katie. A tired, hesitant smile. But what was she thinking? Was she thus resolved?

Lauren and Mary returned with cups of coffee in hand.

"What did y'all do to run David off?" Lauren took her seat beside Tom.

"Nothing I wouldn't do again." Tom winked at his wife.

Wyatt wrapped his hands around the steaming mug and brought it to his lips. He glanced toward the great room where David played with not only Jessie and Peter, but Jack and Susie, as well.

Was it better to be optimistic? Or cautiously expectant, prepared for any number of possibilities?

Or did it all just come down to trusting God?

Ma and Pa had long since left. And it became apparent that David needed to take his sleepy children home. Katherine walked them out to their cart.

David lifted his children one by one into the wagon and then assisted his wife's climb onto the driver's bench.

"Give me a minute," he called up to Mary. "I want to speak to Katherine."

Mary nodded, but her gaze was on the back of the wagon as Jessie and Peter settled in for the ride.

Stepping to Katherine, David set a hand on her back and steered her toward her own porch. He lowered his voice. "I'm sorry about that whole thing with Pa tonight."

She nodded. "It's all right. I don't expect you two to agree on everything. Lord knows, *that*'s not going to happen."

He grinned. "I suppose you're right. We are quite different."

They climbed the steps onto the porch.

"We can't all be the same," Katherine said. "Some of us would be unnecessary."

As they reached the front door, David turned to face her. "Thanks."

"For what?" Why would he thank her? She had sided with Pa more than him. In fact, it was he that pointed out her shortsightedness, same as Pa's.

"You are always, I don't know…a buffer…between me and Pa. More than you know. It gives me the courage to say things I can't otherwise."

She had no idea. He had never seemed tongue-tied. But was that because, as he claimed, she gave him such boldness?

Placing a hand on his upper arm, she said, "I can't imagine that being so. But if it is, you're welcome."

He pulled her into an embrace. "You take care of yourself, you hear?"

She pulled back. "Of course I will."

His features became set and his eyes serious. "Mary told me about the cart that almost ran you over."

"Ah." Katherine nodded. She'd have rather Mary not share so much with David. Nor would she have Mary keep things from her husband if she felt the need to tell him. "It doesn't happen often."

"Katie." His lips fell as he glowered at her. "I mean it."

She sighed. "I know you do. And I love you for it."

He embraced her again and, when he released her, he held her hand for a moment longer. "Go tell Doc you mean to be more careful, too. I think he's even more concerned than I am."

Katherine nodded.

With that, David stepped off the porch, climbed into his family's wagon, and pressed the horse to take them homeward.

And now, she was free to go to bed, but would she? Or were there still words to be had with Wyatt?

Susie fell asleep almost before Wyatt laid her down. Easier than most nights which took a mixture of story and songs to still her energetic body.

Now he took a turn with Jack.

Wyatt created the bedtime story of all stories—with cowboys, a miserly banker, and a thief. Still, Jack wanted for a mystery involving Sherlock Holmes. Wyatt did not think he was up to the task of weaving such a fine tale. Maybe one day.

Tonight, however, there was too much on his mind.

After the story ended, Wyatt rushed through prayers. It wasn't something he liked doing, but his eagerness to get to Katie overcame his better desires.

He turned down Jack's lantern and hobbled into the great

room as the front door shut. Had she just returned after sending David and his family off? Why had it taken so long?

"You all right?" That had to be the most ridiculous question he could have asked. Though she appeared well enough, he knew better.

She looked at him, eyes slightly widened. Was she surprised at his question? Maybe so. "I am. Perhaps a little tired."

"I'm certain you are exhausted." He moved toward her, his gimp leg slowing his progress.

Much to his chagrin, she closed the distance between them. Why could he not be the one in charge?

She put her hands on his arms. "We need to get you off that leg. You'll wear yourself out."

"I might say the same to you." He kept his gaze soft, but the reality of his concern was certain to have shown through.

Nodding, she wrapped an arm around him from his good side. Then, moving forward, she assisted his short walk to their bedroom.

Soon enough, he sat on the edge of their bed. Relief rushed through him as he eased off his limbs, not feeling any more pain in his wounded leg.

"I need to douse the lights." She turned and left the room before he could protest.

But what would he say? He doubted he would be able to force himself back onto his bum leg if he had to.

Moments later, she returned from the now-dark hallway. She moved through the room, turning down the covers and dimming their lantern. He unbuttoned his shirt.

"Here, let me help you into bed." She extended her arms.

He let her assist him as he maneuvered to his side of their mattress.

Then she reached to help with the buttons.

Jerking away, he continued with them himself. "I'm not completely helpless," he reminded her.

"Of course not." She pulled back as if stung. "I only wanted to help."

"I know." He reached out for her, but she was too far away. Why did she do that to him? "I just...I need to do things for myself. Can you understand?"

She nodded.

"Come here." He opened his arms.

Sliding across the mattress's surface, she went into his embrace, laying into his chest.

He held her to himself, relishing the feel of her. "Tell you what...you help me. And I help you."

She sat up and met his gaze. Then nodded. Fingers fell to his shirt's front and worked the rest of the buttons.

Holding his arms out, he plunged his hands into her hair and relieved it of the pins that bound it. He stared into her eyes as the soft waves fell on his lower arms.

Tugging at her gently, he brought her to him for a kiss. They would make it through this strained period.

Because they loved each other.

Because they trusted each other.

And because God was with them.

But for now, he would enjoy his wife.

CHAPTER 4

The Christmas Spirit Went Somewhere

Katherine moved down the main stretch of town. Why was her Christmas spirit so dampened? She was the one who was supposed to bring Yuletide cheer to the whole town, wasn't she? What would happen if she couldn't? Would it be her fault? Would Christmas then be ruined?

And what of her own family? She'd been so busy with everything for the town, she had not taken the time to make their presents.

What would be a good gift for Susie? For Jack? For Wyatt?

Too much to think about.

Too many things. Too many important things.

"Penny for your thoughts?" Mary pressed a hand to Katherine's arm.

"You don't want to hear my thoughts." Katherine shook her head before looking to her companion.

"I do," Mary insisted.

"They just might scare you."

Mary grimaced. "You know better than that."

"We need to get back to this schedule anyway."

Katherine pointed to her task list. "Did you talk to the schoolteacher about the nativity? Did she agree to orchestrate that?"

Silence. Mary chewed on her lip.

"What?" Did everything have to be so exasperating?

"Miss Elston said she would select the parts, but she doesn't want to direct them." Mary cinched her features.

"Doesn't want to direct them?" Katherine bit back.

Mary jerked away.

"Sorry." Katherine pinched the bridge of her nose. "I'm not upset with you. Where, again, did they find this teacher?"

Mary shrugged. "I wasn't on that board."

Katherine forced a breath out through clenched teeth. "Neither was I." But her son was there, even now, learning what he could from this woman. Who apparently couldn't be bothered to direct children in a simple production.

There was no use getting upset or creating trouble over it. Katherine could do it just as well.

And probably do a better job.

That was vanity.

Sorry, Lord.

"You really shouldn't let this upset you so." Mary looped an arm through Katherine's. "Remember, it will only make you tired. And think about what it will do to the baby."

Katherine closed her eyes and took several long breaths. "What am I supposed to do when no one...*no one* in this town seems prepared to help? Everyone wants their own cherished thing to be in the festivities, but they hand it off to me to ensure it's done."

"Breathe. And remember...I'm here!" Mary beamed.

Katherine looked at her sister-in-law and laid a hand on her arm. "And I thank God for you. What would I do without you?"

Mary flushed.

"Speaking of...I need your opinion about something." Katherine put on her best smile.

"What?" Mary seemed skeptical.

"I need some thoughts on presents."

"Oh no..." Mary pulled away. "No, ma'am."

"Please...." Katherine strode after Mary. She just *had* to help with this. If not, Christmas might be ruined!

Wyatt closed Susie's bedroom door with care. He dare not wake the sleeping child. Not after all the effort he had put into getting her to dreamland. How did Katie manage to do that every day? It was such a chore! How much energy could a body so small contain?

A lot, apparently.

His appreciation for Katie's patience had grown in the short time he had cared for Susie on his own.

And to think...Katherine prepared to add an infant to this mayhem in a few weeks. How?

Still, it was that very event—the birth of their child— which drew him, shuffling, out to the barn. Perhaps it wasn't the most secretive place to hide Katie's present, but it had been the best he could come up with. There wasn't anywhere in the house she wouldn't find it. And this far corner of the barn remained untouched most all the time.

The myriad of things piled there were the odds and ends left behind by the Womack family when they abandoned their homestead. And Wyatt couldn't make himself get rid of them, so the darkened corner became a home for these things.

Shouldering his way farther back, he maneuvered through the discarded farm equipment and made his way to the treasured piece.

He lifted a cloth to reveal his handiwork. The smell of the

carved wood filled his nostrils. The piece had yet to be stained or sealed. It remained in its raw form. But it had taken a fine shape. And he hoped Katie would think it as perfect for their child's first bed as he.

Grabbing for a stool, he then sat next to the cradle. He reached forth and ran a hand over the side, relishing the feel of the wood's smooth surface, sanded the last time he ventured back here.

He wished he had been the one to make the cradle all their children spent their first months in. But he didn't begrudge it too much. The cradle brought in with Susie and Jack after their adoption had likely been built by their father or grandfather. That was fitting.

But he sensed that, while Katherine didn't mind the idea of their child bedding down in that piece, she wanted something made for the child. Why she had not mentioned it, he didn't know. Did she fear he would think her petty? That he would find her selfish? Or haughty in some way?

He let his hand lay where their babe's head would rest.

None of these fears were founded. He understood. And wanted the same thing.

One of his greatest fears had always been that he would become his father—hurting Katie or their children. But God had intervened and rescued him. He no longer feared such.

But he determined he would be the kind of father that made every effort, the father that took part in the lives of his children. And, for whatever reason, that meant he wanted his child to sleep in a bed made by his own hands.

Focusing back on the wood, he smiled. Yes, the cradle was ready for stain and seal. The final steps. And he had already selected the proper stain. In fact, hadn't he put the can around here somewhere?

He turned this way and that. Could he see the can from

his position? The stain had been purchased when he started the project...before his injury. Where would he have set it?

There.

The can sat farther away than he'd expected, between an old beaten-up plow and a half-rotted yolk.

He had hidden it well. Almost too well.

How would he reach it? He would have to hobble over there. But how could he reach into the tighter space with his crutch? Curse that thing! How much did he truly need it?

On his feet once more, he all but dragged his leg as he made his way to the can. His confidence grew with each movement forward. Perhaps the day he would manage without the crutch was soon forthcoming. Though, he did find himself leaning against the wall more than he'd like.

That was nothing to be concerned about. The important thing was that he made progress.

Now leaning over the can, he grabbed it up.

Yes, he could do this. He was as independent as ever. He didn't need anyone's help.

The increasing amount of pain in his leg as he made his way back to the stool, unsteady and awkward, told another story. Still, he would count this a victory.

Sitting once more, he put the can on his good leg.

And stared at the lid.

How would he get this open? He had not thought to grab a tool with which to pry it open.

Glancing in the immediate area, he spotted his chisel nearby. He breathed a sigh of relief.

As he reached for it, his balance precarious, the can tipped, almost falling to the floor.

Why must his leg ache so? He wiped at his forehead. Why was he sweating so profusely? This was not difficult. And it would not beat him.

Chisel in hand and the can of stain once again settled on

his good leg, he let out a breath. Time to go to work opening it. If he only had a mallet.

It lay on the opposite side of the cradle.

Dare he set the things he did have to the side and go for the tool he needed? Did he have the stamina left? Would Susie's nap last this long?

He frowned. Was there a way around it?

Maybe he could angle the chisel and use his fist to created the force needed as leverage. It may not be the best plan he'd ever had, but it was his best option at the moment.

Pulling on his injured leg until his knees were parallel, he secured the can between them. He gritted his teeth at the fresh pain shooting through his leg. Why should he acknowledge it? The more he admitted it to himself the more real it was. If he pushed it to the outskirts of his mind, it would lessen, wouldn't it?

He set the chisel's cutting edge between the lid and the lip of the can. And, angling his fist just so, he hit the handle with as much force as he dared.

The blow vibrated through his legs.

He yelped. The lid released as his leg gave way. Turning, the container fell. Despite the pain, he attempted to catch it.

But the can poured out it's contents. His pants, the floor, and even his hand, bore the effects of his miscalculation.

None of that mattered as much as the intensity of the pain coursing through his leg. He cried out, wishing for words that were no longer in his vocabulary.

Why must he be thus infirmed? And just when he saw a glimmer of hope, it was snatched away. Why? Would he be forever plagued by this...this useless limb? To always be a burden? How much longer?

Turning his regard toward heaven, he silently fumed. This Christmas season may be one of remembrance of God's greatest gift to earth; but for Wyatt, it was becoming a struggle to remember that God had his best interest at heart.

Katherine was eager to see her family. She had decided that the town could do without her for the rest of the day.

She wanted the comfort of her husband.

She *needed* the comfort of her husband.

And she longed for the joyfulness of her children.

Not to mention there were things around the homestead to be done. *Numerous* things.

Why did that make her whole body ache? Was she so weak? It was but a few hours past noon. This couldn't be the way of it.

Still, she reminded herself that she carried a heavy load. Not just the weight of the baby, but the responsibility of his or her safety and nourishment. That taxed her body in more ways than she could count.

Wyatt would enumerate them to her well enough if he had any thought about her weariness. Dare she let on to him the depth of her fatigue? Or disguise it? Was that even possible?

Doubtful. Every part of her body seemed sore.

With great effort, she climbed the stairs up to the porch. Had they doubled in number since the last time she had been home?

She paused at the top, setting a hand to her rounded stomach and sucking in breaths. If only she could fill her lungs. But the child made that impossible.

When her body was as satisfied as it could be with what air she could draw in, she stepped to the door. She forced a smile onto her features and opened it.

Silence greeted her.

And an empty house.

What was this? Had Wyatt gone elsewhere and taken Susie? Why? And how?

Was there some emergency forcing him to?

She stilled.

A gentle snoring came from the great room to the right. She turned and spotted Wyatt's dark blond hair peeking out from the back of the armchair.

Stepping toward him, she circled around and approached toward his front. He seemed so peaceful. His features were placid, and his legs had sprawled out somewhat. One hand lay across his stomach and the other had dropped. Below it a book sat askew on the floor.

Ah, so he had tired while reading.

She leaned in, tempted to press her lips to his. Yet as she bent, the movement put extra pressure on the small of her back. Awareness of how unwise this was shot through her.

Jerking back up, she attempted to right herself. Only to lose her balance and pitch forward.

No!

She stuck out her arms to catch herself. An iron grip stilled her.

Icy blue flashed before her.

"Wyatt." She struggled against his hold.

His hands were hard on her, his fingers digging into her flesh. Did he think she attempted to hurt him? *Had* she hurt him?

The steel blue of his eyes softened. "Katie?"

His grip loosened and he shifted as he maneuvered her sideways. Then she sat across his legs, cradled by his arms.

"Are you all right?" She laid a hand to the side of his face, her thumb moving over the grimace on his lips.

"I am well enough. Are you hurt?" His practiced gaze scanned her body.

Her other hand laid over her stomach. "No. I don't think so."

His embrace warmed her. She was tempted to remain there, soaking it in. But something was off.

She met his eyes. "Why did you grip me so hard? Were you having a bad dream?"

He looked toward the fireplace, the muscles in his jaw moving under his skin. "No."

A thinly veiled lie. But would she accomplish anything if she pressed the issue now?

She swallowed. "I should get up. This can't be good for your leg."

He turned to face her once more, tightening his arms around her. "I like you just as you are."

A smile touched her features. "As do I. But we have more to think on than our rathers." She pulled against his arms.

His hold did not relax.

She pushed out a breath and looked at him. "And what must I do, sir, to purchase my freedom?"

Blond brows shot up. "Naught but a kiss, milady."

Angling her head, her lips met his. She moved her hand from his face to his shoulder as his hand moved to her back and pulled her closer.

She broke the kiss for breath. "Please let me relieve your discomfort."

He shook his head slowly, perhaps not in refusal so much as in dissent. That was her assessment.

One of his hands went to her cheek.

She picked it up and pressed a kiss to the palm. But something caught her eye. A splotch on his hand?

Pulling his hand back slightly, she focused on it.

"Something amiss?" His voice felt deep as it vibrated through her body.

"I don't know." She concentrated on his hand. Where was that mark?

She turned the hand over.

"I thought I saw something."

And suddenly, his hand was gone. He had pulled it away.

She looked at him. "What is it?"

"Nothing. Only some dirt. I should wash up." He helped her slide from his lap and onto her feet.

Turning this way and that, she sought out the hand once more. Either hand. But his movements were too quick.

He rose and walked to the sink.

She followed. "Wyatt, what is that on your hands? It doesn't look like dirt. It—"

"I said it's nothing." His voice was light but had a tightness underneath it.

She needed to back off. But why would he be so secretive about something on his hand? It wasn't like him. And she didn't like it.

Not one bit.

Wyatt sat in his dining chair and watched Katie move about the kitchen. He hated himself for it. Why did he let his stained hand keep him from helping? Was the secrecy so important?

He had been charged with keeping track of Susie, but that was a thin cover. Jack did a fine job on his own.

Hadn't he rested plenty today? He'd even secured a nap. And now here was Katie, rushing around after her wearying day, preparing their supper.

She paused by the stove, checked a pot, then took a moment for herself. Lifting a towel to her forehead, she patted at the perspiration that had covered her face. Then she put a hand to her stomach. Was she well?

"Katie…" He rose, leaning on his crutch as he took a step toward her.

Jerking her head in his direction, she held up a hand. "Not one more move, Wyatt Sullivan."

"But—"

"Or one more word." Her eyes flashed. "You will get off that leg if I am forced to tie you down!"

There was no questioning the veracity of her statement. Or the forcefulness behind it. She was intent. It made him wonder which of them was the healer.

But he knew—she was the nurturer of the two of them. And that had developed quickly in her these last couple of years. He dare not challenge it.

As he shrugged, he took his seat once more. Only then did he glance back toward the children.

Jack's wide eyes had followed their interaction.

Wyatt wasn't so proud that he minded his son seeing him bend to his wife's better judgment. Perhaps it was a good thing for Jack to see—that the boy's mother cared and could sometimes be wiser.

As the tension stilled and dissipated between him and Katie, Jack returned to his play with Susie.

Now Wyatt didn't know where to direct his eyes. Should he continue watching Katie? Or would she fear he scrutinized her every move? Perhaps he should mind Jack and Susie's playtime. He passed the next several moments with his attention on them.

They were endearing. It was difficult to imagine that they had almost been separated from each other after their mother died. If Katie hadn't been so stubborn, and cared more about them than her own desires, they wouldn't be together right now.

Thank God for her stubbornness.

A whimper came from the kitchen.

Wyatt whipped his head around.

Katie's arms were wrapped around her midsection as she hunched over the edge of the sink, her face a contorted mess of pain.

"What?" He was on his feet, pushing forward as fast as he could manage.

She looked at him, but as she opened her mouth, a cry escaped.

Muttering a curse, he dropped the crutch and dragged his leg, ignoring the searing heat coursing through it.

As he came upon her, his arms went around her.

She clung to his shirt. Tears flowed. "I...don't know...what is happening."

He saw the naked fear in her eyes.

Could she see it in his? He fought to put up that mask, the one he wore when he entered terrifying, life-threatening situations. But in that moment, it seemed impossible to raise it. Panic took hold of him at his very core, surrounding his heart, squeezing it.

But he couldn't give way to it. That wouldn't help the situation. Someone had to remain calm. He needed to get Katie to her bed. And he couldn't do it alone.

"Jack," he called.

The boy appeared at Wyatt's elbow.

Jack's eyes were wider than before.

Wyatt put a hand on his shoulder. "I need you to be brave."

Jack nodded.

"We must get Ma to her bed."

Jack bobbed his head again, a single motion.

"Can you help her? Let her lean on you?"

Susie cried then. There was no way to hide the uneasiness in the room. And she could sense it.

He would have to deal with that later. Right now, Katie needed his full attention.

K atherine opened her eyes. All was still. What had happened?

The baby!

Putting hands to her stomach, she breathed out her relief at the swell of her child.

She whispered a prayer of gratitude and did not try to stop the tears that fell.

"Katie," a soft voice said as the mattress gave a little to the side.

Closing her eyes, she took in the comfort of her husband's love.

Wyatt wiped her tears and smoothed a hand over her hair.

"Wh-what happened?" She shuddered.

He sighed and continued stroking her hair.

Opening her eyes once more, she sought his gaze.

His piercing blue eyes were fixed on her face. There was peace there for her. But also turmoil. Was everything well?

"Wyatt?" Her voice rose. She lifted her head.

"Be still, love. Don't try to move." His tone remained flat. It did not invite discussion.

Her lip trembled. There was something he wasn't telling her.

His brows furrowed. "Don't fret so." He leaned down and kissed first her forehead and then her lips.

Neither distracted her, however, from what might have occurred. Was that his purpose?

As he pulled back, her gaze caught and held his. "Wyatt." She drew in another long breath and blinked.

Realization hit her. Her baby hadn't moved since she awoke.

"Please." Tears threatened to overcome her again. Could she even try to fight them? "Tell me."

His eyes softened. "You went into labor."

She bit her lip. But that did not stop her shaking.

He rubbed her arms. "I was able to stop it."

"The...baby?" It took a moment for her to force the word out.

"There is no reason to think the baby is unwell." His words were a lifeline. She clung to them.

"Truly?"

He nodded. Was there moisture welling in his eyes? They shone.

"But..." She licked her lips. Why was her mouth so dry? "I haven't felt the baby move."

No hint of surprise registered in Wyatt's features. Why? What did he know? She appreciated his tenderness, but she would go crazy, for certain, if he didn't come out with it.

"The baby may be resting from the labor. He or she needs sleep, too." His mouth turned up at the corners. But the smile didn't reach his eyes.

She didn't find it comforting.

He intertwined their fingers. Why did his eyes display such sorrow if everything was truly all right? Dare she enter that place or continue as she was, in ignorance?

That would not work for her.

"If we are well as you say, then why does your face tell a different story?"

He drew in a long breath and released it slowly. Then he moved closer to her. "Can you imagine how afraid I was?"

She kept her eyes latched to his. He? Was afraid?

"I..." He choked. With emotion? Was he so caught up? "I could have lost you." He squeezed her hand.

She held his with a firmness that defied her condition.

"And our baby."

Nodding, she felt more tears making their way down her face. Still, there was hope. "But you are a good doctor."

The light in his eyes dimmed. "I've lost patients before. Even infants."

What could he mean?

"I can do everything right and still lose laboring women. And their babies. It's happened before." His voice seemed hollow. That was the doctor taking over.

Did he know with certainty that he had done what he could? That even he couldn't save everyone.

But now the husband and father saw it from a new perspective.

She reached a hand to his face, touching his cheek. "I knew you wouldn't let me die."

He jerked away. "Those are fine words, but I am powerless to honor them. I'm not God."

Her hand dropped and she felt the full foolishness of her statement. How childish, how strange they seemed to her now. And she couldn't un-speak them.

How many hours passed before Katie fell into blissful sleep? It was best. How had he been able to hold himself together? But he had been determined not to give in to his emotions as he held her hand, caressed her face, her hair.

Now that she slept, he found himself in desperate need of respite. Only...

The children.

Jack had calmed Susie and put her to bed. His eyes had been so worn, so tired when Wyatt informed him the danger was past. Had he then gone to bed, as well?

Hobbling the few steps down the hall to Jack's room, he pushed the door open just a crack. A light illuminated the room. Jack sat on his bed, poring over one of his books. He didn't even look up at the sound of the door hinges squeaking.

"Jack," Wyatt whispered into the quietness.

The lad's head popped up. "Pa? Everything all right?" Fear marred the boy's expression.

"Yes." Wyatt held a hand up to still the boy. "Ma is well. I just...wanted to thank you for your help. And tell you it's time for some shut-eye."

Jack nodded. He placed a bookmark between his book pages and set the volume to the side. Then, reaching up and putting the lantern out, he maneuvered farther under the covers.

Why didn't Wyatt just back away and leave the youngster to his rest? Did he have more to say? Searching his heart, he was uncertain of himself.

Jack leaned up on an elbow and faced the doorway. "Pa?"

"Yeah, Jack?" Had the boy sensed Wyatt's hesitation?

"Did you need something?" The boy's features were diffi-cult to read.

So Jack had noticed his hesitation. What did the boy think caused it?

Wyatt opened the door wider and stepped through, allowing light from the hall to spill in and illuminate his path.

Sitting on the edge of Jack's bed, he measured out his

words. "The way you helped with your Ma and your sister tonight..." Wyatt's voice broke.

Jack nodded. "I know, Pa."

"You made me proud." He wanted to press his mouth into a smile for Jack, but it wouldn't come.

The boy fidgeted with his fingers.

Wyatt lowered his brows. "Something wrong?"

"I just...I don't want you to think..."

Reaching out to Jack, Wyatt put a hand to his shoulder. "You're my son. Nothing could make me think of you any different."

Jack's gaze met Wyatt's. Were his eyes glazed?

"I just...I was so scared." Jack dropped his head.

Wyatt opened his arms and Jack fell into them. "There's no shame in that. It was a scary situation."

He continued to hold his son for several moments, letting the lad take comfort from him.

"Can I tell you something?"

Jack nodded against his shoulder.

"I was scared, too. More scared than I've been in my whole life."

The boy pulled back. "You were?"

"I was." Wyatt fought back the intense emotions threatening to overwhelm him. "It could have gone badly. For your Ma. And for the baby."

"But you knew what to do." Jack seemed confused.

"I wasn't certain it would work. There have been times I've used all my skill and still lost a patient."

Jack remained silent, his eyes widening.

"It's true. Doctors can't fix everyone. That kind of power only belongs to God." Wyatt mused on the same words he had spoken to Katie earlier.

"But why would God let people die?"

"That, my boy, is a big question. Much bigger than we can get through in a bedtime discussion."

Jack's face fell.

"It's one of those things we may never understand. But that's why we have faith. Why we trust that He is God *and* He is good."

The boy looked at his father. As Wyatt watched, that familiar light in Jack's affect returned. A measure of peace seemed to cover Wyatt's soul.

"Now," Wyatt said, catching Jack's eyes, "I best say good night. I think we both need rest—"

A knock sounded on the front door, echoing through the house.

Who would be calling at this hour? And why?

Jack and Wyatt exchanged a look. The boy's expression mirrored Wyatt's own trepidation.

"Lay down. I'll see who it is."

Jack nodded slowly and with hesitation, but he obeyed.

Wyatt stood and hobbled from the room, closed the bedroom door, and maneuvered toward the front door, with painstakingly slow steps.

Should he grab his gun? The rifle leaned against the wall by the door. Had Katie set it there for just such an occasion after he became injured? He must remember to thank her for her forethought later.

The knock sounded again.

"Doc? Katie?"

Wyatt knew that voice—David Matthews.

As he approached the door, Wyatt paused and let out a breath, trying to release the tension building in his shoulders. But only for a moment.

Why would David come? And so late? Was someone hurt? Needing his care?

Closing the few remaining steps to the door, he opened it

to reveal his brother-in-law. The man's features scrunched in an unpleasant way. Was he upset?

"What's the matter?" Wyatt put on the doctor without effort.

David shouldered his way in. "Mary told me that Katie wasn't well earlier today. I just had to check on her."

That was it? Did David not trust Wyatt to care for Katie? Wyatt's shoulders stiffened and a defensive ire rose in him. But he remembered—he would have to tell David about the evening's happenings. Would he then earn the man's distrust?

"She is well. Resting." Best to stick to the facts. And keep the interchange to a minimum.

David turned on him. His gaze fell hard on Wyatt. "Truly? Mary is concerned she's overworked and overstressed."

Wyatt let out a breath but turned away. He couldn't let David read the guilt on his features. "I agree. She has taken on too much."

The intensity of David's glare did not abate.

Closing his eyes, Wyatt admitted, "And my condition does not help the matter." How could he face David's judgment? How could he face his own?

David let out a breath. "It's a tough situation...certainly. But we can't let her overdo it."

Wyatt met David's gaze then. "Do you know who you're talking about? Have you ever tried to dissuade your sister from something she wants to do? Or feels obligated to?"

Shrugging, David relaxed his features. "Many times. But that's not *my* responsibility." His gaze leveled on Wyatt once more.

Would the man not give Wyatt any leeway?

"So, she's resting?" David scanned the great room and dining area. He paused. Had something caught his attention?

He shot a disturbed look at Wyatt as he stepped toward the kitchen.

As David stood in front of the stove, he lifted lids from pots of food long gone cold.

Wyatt grimaced. There was no way he could stop the progression of this conversation.

"Is there a reason dinner didn't happen as planned?" David's eyes were hard.

Wyatt had two choices—continue to offer only what details he must or be more forthcoming about the evening's events.

Sighing, his decision made, he spoke, "Katie went into labor."

David's regard went from questioning to accusatory.

Why? Had he always lived on the edge of judgment toward Wyatt?

"Is she—?" He stepped toward the hall.

Wyatt, having made steady movements, was now in David's path. "She is well. I was able to stop it. Both she and our child are fine."

For whatever reason that did nothing to alter the harshness of David's gaze. When he did speak, his words accused. "Perhaps I should send for Dr. Brown."

Wyatt jerked away. "Why?"

"To ensure Katie and the baby are safe," David spoke simply, his expression impassive.

Why would he think Wyatt incapable? "I don't understand."

David didn't answer but continued to watch Wyatt as he stepped closer.

"Are you saying that you doubt my abilities as a doctor? Or my care as a husband?" Wyatt flared his nostrils. He wanted to keep his anger in check, but it became rather difficult. There could be no good answer to this question. Not from this man whose good opinion he had trusted.

"I know you love Katie. I don't think you would ever

intentionally do anything to hurt her." David's tone was flat and his words measured.

"Then…you question my capability as a physician." It was not a question. And though the words were spoken plainly, they marred Wyatt's spirit.

David looked at the floor.

Some moments passed.

Would the man answer?

Just when Wyatt decided that he would not receive a response, David let out a sigh.

"I don't want what befell Millie to happen to my sister."

Wyatt wouldn't have been more wounded if David had flung a dagger.

Millie.

The woman he'd lost in childbirth last year.

She went into premature labor. So early. Too early.

But she hadn't Katie's constitution. There had been complications. *Plenty* of complications.

And though Wyatt had done everything he could, the woman and child had died.

Was he truly satisfied that he had done what he could? Yes.

Did the deaths still plague him? Yes. Every death on his watch did no matter his skill as a physician.

When Wyatt looked at David again, his brother-in-law faced the great room. What could he say? Was there anything to say? How could he defend himself?

"I…am sorry you feel that way."

David set hands to his hips and shook his head. "Is that all the sympathy you have for Millie?"

Wyatt looked up, refusing to turn away from David's glare. "Of course not. I carry that loss with me every day."

One of David's eyebrows quirked. Had that surprised him? Did he think Wyatt so cold and unfeeling?

"In every situation, I do everything I can for my patient. Everything. Even so, I grieve that I couldn't save her."

David's features softened. "I guess I know that. But…"

Wyatt waited for him to continue.

"She's my baby sister."

"I understand that." Wyatt nodded. "And she's my wife."

"Millie was Jonas's wife." David's voice broke.

And Wyatt remembered. Millie had been married to David's good friend, Jonas, a fellow miner who had been through much with David. Even that day, David had been there, waiting and praying with Jonas. He'd stood by Jonas when the news of Millie's passing came. How had that detail slipped by him?

The pieces fit more clearly now.

"I am sorry your friend is grieving. You must know that if there was anything…*anything* I could do or could have done, I would have."

David nodded. "I do."

Wyatt watched his brother-in-law relax into his frame a bit more.

The man's eyes avoided Wyatt's. "I apologize for saying that you—"

"It is forgotten." Wyatt waved a hand.

David looked down the hall in the direction of Wyatt and Katie's bedroom. "I'd like to see her, but I don't want to disturb her sleep."

"I do think she needs all the rest she can get." Wyatt stood straighter despite his crutch.

"I'll be on my way then." David turned to the door. Then he spun back. "Can I come tomorrow?"

"Of course." Wyatt smiled. "She'll be under strict orders to stay in bed, but she'd love to see you."

David nodded, then spun and let himself out.

Wyatt didn't make a move to secure the door. Not yet. He

shifted to the right and sank into his armchair and...just for a moment, let himself fall apart.

Katherine sat in bed, sulking. She had been so busy this past month that this whole resting business had her completely bored.

But Wyatt looked out for her and their child's best interest as a physician and a father. She had no doubts his assertions had been for her own good.

Still, she had stared at these walls for hours now. Hours!

Wyatt and Susie came in and out as Susie allowed, but the toddler didn't care to be cooped up in here any more than Katherine did.

A couple of books sat on the nightstand, but neither was as intriguing or as satisfying as her moping. Yes, she had turned it into quite the pastime. And in just a morning's span of time. Imagine what the next couple of weeks would bring.

Argh!

A sound echoed in the quietness of the room. What was it?

Aaagh!

There it was again. Did someone knock on her door?

"Come in?" she called.

Oh, please, let it be Wyatt coming to sit with me!

The door latch moved.

Thank You, Lord!

An opening appeared between the frame and the door, but the face that greeted her was not that of her husband, but of her sister-in-law.

"Mary!" Katherine was so thrilled she might just cry.

"Katie?" Mary whispered. "You awake?"

"Unfortunately," Katherine muttered. One could only sleep so much.

"What was that?" Had Mary not heard her comment? Probably for the best.

"I am. Please, come in," Katherine encouraged her to come in farther.

Soon enough, Mary slipped into the room and stood at the bed's edge. But instead of delight upon her features, her mouth and eyes were etched with concern.

"Please don't worry so," Katherine pressed. "I am well enough. I promise."

"Truly?" Mary's eyes glazed with moisture.

Katherine put a hand to her stomach. "Yes. We both are."

Mary threw her arms around Katherine. "Praise be to God!" The embrace was sweet, but maybe a bit more smothering than Katherine would have liked. Still, she dare not breathe a word about it.

"Yes. I thank God that Wyatt was here."

Pulling back, Mary sniffled and wiped at her eyes. "Katie, I am so, so sorry."

Katherine furrowed her brows. "For what?"

Mary fell into the seat that Wyatt had sat in throughout the day. "For not helping you more. You were overwhelmed with the town Christmas traditions. I saw that. And I should have taken care of more things."

Laying a hand on Mary's, Katherine gave her a stern look. "Now listen to me, *I* pushed myself. I took on that project. You did everything I asked and then some. No one is to blame for my being overworked but me."

Mary nodded.

"And whoever injured Wyatt."

"Have they found the rogue?" Mary's eyes flashed.

Katherine shook her head. "No. And the sheriff said they were not able to find any leads. They've given up."

Mary looked at her hands. She seemed so forlorn.

"What is it?" Katherine settled a hand over hers again.

"I am just...see I...well, I was so worried, Katie. And when your brother told me what happened last night, I couldn't hardly sleep for thinking what I should have done better."

"Now you stop that right now. Not only is it not true, thinking about what could have or should have been, doesn't help anyone, does it?" Katherine's tone hardened.

"No, I suppose not." Mary smiled.

"Good." Katherine returned the grin. "Let's not speak of it again."

"Agreed." Mary squeezed Katherine's hand.

Katherine leaned her head against the backboard and closed her eyes. She was thankful for her brother and his wife. They cared so much for her and her little family that they would rush over here after—

She opened her eyes.

"Did you say David told you last night?"

"Yes," Mary said, reaching to the nightstand to fill Katherine's water. "Right after he returned from visiting Wyatt."

David? Came here? And talked with Wyatt? Why, then, hadn't Wyatt shared as much with her?

"Something amiss?" Mary asked as she held the glass out to Katherine.

"I'm not sure." Katherine took the cup and drank. "But I should speak with my husband."

CHAPTER 6

Silent Night

I t had been a long day. Katherine stayed in bed, and more people had paraded through her bedroom in this one day than in these last two years combined. First Mary and David came, then Ma and Pa. And the children. So many children ran around her bed.

But it became quiet. The extended family left. And now she could speak with Wyatt.

Except he busied himself putting Susie and Jack to bed.

Katherine waited with every ounce of patience she could muster. She did so tire of her confinement. Regardless of the sense of it. Regardless that it was for the safety of her baby.

It didn't mean she had to like it, did it?

And while Wyatt's delay gave her time to gather her thoughts, she found the waiting difficult. Why had Wyatt not spoken of David's visit late last night? Perhaps it was nothing, but she found it curious. The very fact that he had been remiss in telling her made her suspicious. And concerned.

The door opened.

Wyatt shuffled in. His hobbling more and more of late became a shuffling. She trusted that his leg had been healing well. And she hoped the recent change in his workload would not hamper his recovery. Could she forgive herself if it did?

He lifted his gaze to hers. The tiredness was evident in his features. Had this day worn on him also? Perhaps even more than it had her?

Maybe she should delay their conversation.

But the longer she did so, the larger it would grow in her mind. That would not serve either of them.

"How are you?" Wyatt huffed out as he moved to his side of the bed.

"I am well." She rubbed her hands across her oversized stomach. "A bit worn with these four walls."

He set his crutch down and all but fell upon the bed, shaking her.

"I understand that." Reaching out his hand, he laid his atop hers on their child.

Just then, the baby kicked at their joined hands.

Wyatt lifted his head and caught Katherine's gaze. Amusement lit the blue in his eyes, making them sparkle. "He's eager to meet his ma."

She smiled. "So a boy for certain?"

Wyatt shifted to his side, facing her. He shrugged. "That's what I've always thought. You have any feelings one way or another?"

Looking toward her abdomen, she wondered. Had she considered it? Thought of their baby in one direction or the other?

Turning back to him, she smiled. "I can't say I have a strong leaning either way."

He bent forward and pressed a kiss to her hands, still on her stomach. So tender. So loving.

She slid her hand out and brushed his hair back. "How are you?"

He seemed to ignore her, feeling along the different angles of her stomach. Was he searching for more movement?

"You did have a difficult task today, hosting the horde of well-wishers."

"Mary was the hostess today. I spent most of my time assuring your ma that you and the baby are well enough." The weight of it seemed to fall on him in that moment. He pulled back and landed once more on his pillow.

Katherine shifted and leaned over him, pressing a hand to his chest. "I'm sorry. But they know you'll take good care of me. They just worry."

He didn't respond.

"Sweetheart?" She stretched her legs out even farther so she could lay beside him.

"Yeah?" His gaze remained on the ceiling.

She would get to the core of his distress. "Is something troubling you?"

He ran a hand down his face.

"Tell me," she insisted.

Turning toward her, his eyes shone in the dimness. "I don't want to worry you with things that need not concern you."

She paused. What was that supposed to mean? Was there more to that statement than seemed on the surface? One thing she knew—she couldn't let it go at that. "I'm still your partner. And we agreed to do life together. The fact that I'm pregnant does not change that, does it?"

He reached for her face, cupping her cheek. "I want to protect you, not burden you."

She stiffened. A fire lit within her. "I'm not made of glass, Wyatt Sullivan. I should think you of all people would know that."

His hand dropped. "I've upset you."

She thinned her lips as she met his gaze with heat in her own.

"That was not my intention." He shifted to his side again and pushed out a breath. "All right."

She relaxed, the tension in her shoulders releasing.

He searched her features, then lifted a hand and ran fingers through her hair, still loose from her ordeal the night before. Was he stalling?

"Your brother came by last night after..."

She nodded. He need not speak of the incident.

He let his hand fall to the mattress and he looked past her. Did he attempt to catch his memory? Or to measure his words?

Wyatt sighed. "He wasn't too pleased."

Katherine furrowed her brows. "Not pleased? With you? Why ever not?"

Wyatt met Katherine's eyes. "He thought we should turn to Dr. Brown to monitor your care."

That couldn't be right. Why wouldn't David trust Wyatt? "Surely you misunderstood."

The blue of Wyatt's eyes became steely. "I am certain I did not."

Katherine hated this invisible barrier between them. But how could he be serious?

Her brother? Not trust Wyatt? That didn't make sense. She would either trust her husband and take him at his word or reject his account.

Which would it be?

With her free hand, she touched the side of Wyatt's face. "Tell me what happened."

"Wyatt!"

Someone called to him, the voice cutting through the haze of his sleep. He opened his eyes. Time to get to work. If someone needed him, he had to wake up.

"Wyatt!"

It was Katie.

The baby!

He jerked upright, laying a hand to his wife. Only she was no longer beside him.

Where could she be?

Everything was dark. And hot. And smelled of smoke.

"Katie!"

"Wyatt," she cried. "The house. It's on fire."

He was on his feet in a moment. Tempted to reach for the crutch, he quickly dismissed the idea. That would only slow him. He could walk through the pain. "Get Susie. I'll get Jack."

How bad was it? How much had it consumed? Had it spread to the barn? Or started there?

As he moved around the bed, he saw her silhouette maneuver out the bedroom door.

"Katie!" he called.

She turned.

"Cover your nose and mouth with a cloth and crouch as much as you can."

Her head bobbed and she tore at the sleeve of her nightgown.

He turned his attention to his own hem. Ripping off a piece, he covered the lower portion of his face and moved toward Jack's room.

His steps were pained, but he pushed through and, seconds later, shoved the door open.

Jack lay in bed, coughing.

Wyatt rushed into the room, his teeth clenched against the

stabbing sensation in his leg. If they didn't get out, it didn't matter what happened to his leg.

Shaking his son, he ripped a piece of sheet from the bed linens.

Jack woke, sputtering. How much smoke had he taken into his lungs?

Wyatt pressed the cloth over Jack's nose.

The boy fought against him.

"It's all right, Jack. It's me—Pa. There is danger. You need to breathe through this. And we have to get out of the house. Now."

The roof cracked above him. That couldn't be good.

Grabbing Jack's shoulders, Wyatt urged the boy to his feet.

Jack stumbled, but righted himself.

"Go!" Wyatt yelled.

The boy's movements were slower than Wyatt liked, but Jack was going nonetheless.

Unnerving sounds continued to fill Wyatt's ears. The fire must have been raging for some time. Would any part of the house survive? Wyatt was doubtful.

But none of that mattered if his family made it to safety.

Stepping into the hall, another form moved their way. A shriek filled Wyatt with relief. Katie and Susie lived.

Herding them to go before him, he pressed Katie and Jack to move.

The sound of splitting wood became louder. He looked back. The place where the hall had been was gone. Flames licked at the remains.

"Go!" he shouted.

His leg had become useless, he now dragged it behind. But he became more certain they would make it out of the house. He prayed that there they would find safety.

What of the horses?

He had to worry about his family first.

When the roof above him splintered, there was no possibility of moving out of the way.

He looked after his wife and children, several paces ahead, nearly to the door.

Thank You, Lord. Take care of them.

The ceiling collapsed behind Katherine. She pulled Jack farther away.

"Wyatt!" Katherine turned and screamed.

Her instincts told her to run to him, to help him...but the children.

She handed a crying Susie to Jack. "Go! Out of the house. Now!"

"But, Ma..." Jack choked out.

"No. Get Susie and yourself to safety." Tears streamed down her face. But she didn't have time for them. Or for Jack's sentiments. She had to do what she could, if she could do anything, to save Wyatt.

Jack's body shook as he gathered his sister to himself and ran for the front door.

Once he was out of sight, Katherine turned back toward the heap that been the large space between the dining table and great room.

Where was her beloved?

"Wyatt!"

The rubble moved.

She rushed for that section of the smoking mess. Wyatt was there, pushing pieces of roofing off his body. But his legs remained buried.

Kneeling, she jerked on this and that. She had to free him.

A firm hand grabbed her arm.

Her gaze lifted to Wyatt's.

His mouth opened. He yelled at her. "...too dangerous... must...go..."

She shook her head. "I'm not leaving you."

He jerked both of her hands off the rubble. "Go!"

Hot tears poured from her. How could she leave him to die? Still, she couldn't fight that he was right. She had to protect their child, to be there tomorrow for them. What would happen to them if both she and Wyatt perished?

She jerked her hands until she held his. Then, leaning forward, she pressed her lips on his. Would this be their last kiss?

Hands pulled at her from behind. Had Jack returned? The pull was strong.

Her body fell against the form. The figure was much taller than her son.

"Go, Katie. I've got this."

David!

How did he know?

It mattered not. His chances of rescuing Wyatt were much greater. She twisted and met his gaze.

"I promise."

Nodding, she pulled herself up and rushed for the door.

Her little family stood several feet from the homestead. When she turned, a heaviness settled in the base of her stomach. She felt sick at the sight. The home was a loss. Flames engulfed most of the structure. But the barn seemed untouched. Would they be able to stop the fire before it spread?

Time passed sluggishly as she waited to spy her brother and husband. She sent up a million prayers.

Hoof beats upon the dirt road drew her attention. Several men came, her father at the lead. Salvation!

Thank You, Lord!

Another section of roof collapsed.

No!

She stepped toward the structure.

Jack jerked at her shoulder. He *was* stronger than she'd thought.

Her Pa didn't bother tying off his horse. He dropped and ran for the house, pausing only briefly by Katherine. "Where are they?"

"I-in the great room." Her voice trembled.

Pa stepped to the porch steps. Was there any hope?

Two figures emerged from the front door. One bearing the other over his shoulder as the second limped.

She cried out. Could God be so good?

Nothing. She would never ask for anything again.

Her husband and brother were alive.

Wyatt stirred. He became aware that Katherine's warm body lay beside him.

The events of the previous evening swept over him as he neared full awareness. And with the memories, came a multitude of questions.

How had the fire started? Had the barn been spared? The horses? What was the state of the property?

The townsfolk had come to their aid and had secured him and his family to the clinic's recovery rooms. Therein, lay the second place his thoughts turned—how thankful he was for God's hand of provision and protection.

As he looked at the sleeping form of his wife, emotion welled in his throat until it ached. They had almost lost each other. Forever.

But for David's intervention...

How had he known about the fire? Such that he would arrive at just the right moment?

Coincidence? Wyatt had pretty much dismissed all belief in coincidences long ago.

A stiffness in his knee gave way to a desire to shift. However, the moment he did so, he regretted it. Fresh pain in his leg tore through him. How had he endured such injury and walked, or limped, out of the house on his own feet?

Katie moved beside him.

He wrapped an arm around her and pulled her closer. Would he ever let go? Pressing a kiss to the side of her face, he became aware that she rose to alertness.

Turning her head, she met his gaze. "Wyatt?" Her voice was gruff, dry, and scratched from the smoke.

"Yes, my love?" He stroked her hair, pulling strands back from her face.

"The house...is it...?" Her eyes filled.

She knew.

He took her hand and lifted it to his chest. Would her touch give him the comfort he craved? "Yes, darling. It's gone."

Tears slipped through her guard and down her face.

His handiwork, hours put into building a home for him and this little family were gone. In a matter of hours. Still, there was more to be grateful for. "But we are all well enough. Jack and Susie are in recovery rooms. Sleeping. Safe."

She nodded, but that did nothing to stop her tears. There must be a lot of emotion stuffed between her slender shoulders.

Even his broader ones did not seem capable of holding it.

"What will we do?" Her voice shook.

"We'll stay here." He met her gaze. "Until we find another home or I can rebuild."

"Rebuild?" Was that confusion or hopefulness in her voice? His own feelings clouded his ability to read hers.

"If that's what you'd like."

She turned away, facing the window. Even with the curtains drawn, it allowed bits of light in. After pulling in a deep breath, she let loose a long sigh. "But where will we have Christmas?"

"Katie, you know Christmas is more than a tree or a place. We can celebrate Christ's birth anywhere. Without all this to-do. All we need is each other." He set a hand on her shoulder. "And thank God we have that."

But she remained silent. Had this fire damaged more than their house?

CHAPTER 7

We Need A Little Christmas

Their blissful sleep couldn't last forever. Katherine and her family had to pull themselves together and get out of bed to face the day. A day full of unknowns. Would they find the answers they sought?

Jack and Susie played in the room next door. With what, Katherine wasn't certain and she wasn't sure she wanted to know.

Katherine had been shooed out of the room she and Wyatt shared so Dr. Brown could look at the newly acquired injuries.

She stepped into the only empty room—the one Susie used. Fresh water sat in a bucket by the vanity. Who had procured it for her? Pouring some into the basin there took more effort than she'd expected due to the size of the bucket. But as she splashed the cool liquid on her face and washed her hands, Katherine relished the feeling of being clean.

Looking down, she realized that the blue gingham was the only dress she had now. It wasn't even her favorite. For whatever reason, that seemed hard to swallow. How petty could she be? Her family survived the massive fire and here she was bemoaning the loss of her dresses.

She focused back on the now dirty water. At least she had removed most of the dirt and soot from her exposed skin. Moving to the bed, she sat and pulled back her hair. A bun? Or a braid?

Her arms ached as she held them over her shoulders. No, she hadn't the patience for anything elaborate. A simple braid would have to do.

How much longer would Dr. Brown be with Wyatt? Was the lengthy duration of the exam a good sign? Or something she should be concerned about? Why lie to herself with false hope? From her experience, the time dragging by didn't bode well.

She shook her head. It *would* be all right. Wyatt was alive and well. They could overcome whatever wounds he had incurred. And he would resume his recovery from the shotgun blast. They would do it together.

Knock, knock, knock.

Katherine's heart leapt. Dr. Brown must be done with Wyatt. Could she see him now?

She took in a lungful of air. Now they would tell her how Wyatt's recovery would be.

Was she ready?

She had to be.

When she opened the door, however, she was not facing the doctor from Victor, but her father.

"Pa?" Had something gone terribly wrong? Did they send Pa in to tell her? "What's happened to Wyatt?"

His gaze held hers, and his brows gathered. "Wyatt?"

Was he confused?

"Dr. Brown...did he send you to tell me something?" Her heart raced. Could she endure much more?

"No, Katie. I ain't been to see Dr. Brown. I came looking for you." He reached for her hand.

Her breaths came in and out rapidly.

"I think you best sit yourself down."

She narrowed her eyes. It seemed he did have unfortunate tidings. Nodding, she let her father lead her to the bed. After sitting, she watched as Pa moved a chair closer to her and sat.

"W-why did you come, Pa?" She couldn't keep the trembling from her words. But she faced him with boldness she couldn't fathom she still had.

"Can't a man be concerned after his daughter? Want to make sure with his own eyes that she's well?"

"Of course." Her lip twitched on one side. "But there's more, isn't there? I sense you are holding something back."

His eyes searched hers. "I never could hide anything from you."

She shook her head. "You'd best get it out. I can take it." Clasping her hands on top of her knees, she braced herself.

"You know that no matter what, we're in this together, right? Family is everything."

What was he saying? She worked out his words, trying to unearth the hidden meaning in them. Something in the pit of her stomach cinched and a fearful trepidation filled the core of her being. Could she stop it from spreading?

"Your brother, he—"

"Just tell it." She pressed her words out, perhaps harsher than she'd intended. "What's David to do with all of this?"

"He rang the alarm last night." Pa's voice quieted and stilled for a moment.

So David rang the alarm. What was Pa not saying?

"It was he that saved Wyatt. And kept the fire from spreading."

"That's true," she said, dragging out the word.

Pa hung his head.

"Pa..." Why was he so bothered? So David rang the alarm after...

What? How could David have known? Unless...

Her father did not look up. She became desperate for his eyes. How was she supposed to read him without them? The world began to spin. But she fought for clarity.

"Pa, how did David know about the fire?" Heat flushed through her. But what form did it take? Rage? Shame? Both? What had David done?

"He had a visitor."

What? The pieces were jumbled in her mind. Nothing made sense. "A visitor?"

Pa nodded and licked his lips. "Jonas came to David's home and told him about the fire."

"Jonas...?" The blood drained from Katherine's face. She needn't ask how Jonas knew. Pa's insinuation was clear.

Jonas had set fire to her house.

But why? Had he not forgiven Wyatt for the death of his wife and child. Held a grudge? To this extent? Was Jonas, the gentle soft-spoken friend of her brother's, capable of this? Of putting her family in danger?

Her stomach twisted painfully. Their home. Their beautiful home...gone. Because of the bitter root in Jonas's heart? The ache in her chest for her family's loss clouded her mind.

But one thing rose to the surface—if Jonas set the fire, why would he warn David? A guilty conscience?

Had he decided that he didn't, in fact, want to murder her and her children in their sleep?

She laid her head in her hands. For some moments she let her thoughts chase each other and swirl in her mind.

These pieces shouldn't fit, but they did.

"Where..." she gasped. "Where is Jonas now?"

"In jail." Pa frowned. Now the naked anger clouded over his features. He raged at the man, too. "The townsfolk tracked him down after the fire was put out."

Relief washed over her. Jonas wouldn't be able to change his mind and attempt to bring about their demise. Or her husband's. Was Jonas…? Could he have been the one who shot Wyatt?

She lifted her head. "Pa, do you think—?"

He put a hand to her shoulder. "Don't dwell on it, Katie. There's no sense in it."

"But what if—?" She needed to know. She *had* to know.

"He's in jail. Where he will remain until his trial."

It wasn't right. Why should he get away with trying to kill her husband now twice? Would he only answer for the fire?

"The man has lost his wife and his child. Now, he's lost his freedom and possibly what life he had. He deserves our pity. Not our vengeance."

Katherine wasn't certain she could extend that kind of grace. When she closed her eyes, she saw the roof collapse on her husband. *Every* time she closed her eyes.

How could she move on? How could she forgive?

Would Wyatt ever return to full health? How long must he suffer with this leg?

He should be thankful that it carried him out of the burning house. That he was alive.

Still, he couldn't help but bemoan the weeks of infirmary he had endured. And the burden it had placed on Katie, leading to the premature labor.

All that worrying.

And, finally, he begrudged his inability to get them away from danger quicker.

Yes, it all fell on him.

Katie worked over him even now. She cleaned his wound and changed the bandage. Her full midsection made her efforts all the more difficult.

She shouldn't be taxed with such. This was his job—

seeing to the wounds of the town, the ills, the ailments. But he hadn't been much good for anyone lately, least of all his family.

He tensed as she tightened the cloth around the reddened, sore mid-calf.

"Did I hurt you?" Her eyes flashed to his.

"Don't worry. It is only a bit tender." He examined her from the top of her head down. Was he now no more than a cripple to her? Someone she had to care for?

He caught himself. That line of thinking wouldn't lead anywhere good. Besides, he knew better. She loved him. Truly. And while she tended to him now, he had cared for her only days before.

There was, after all, a give and take.

In his heart, he found that he didn't like this aspect of marriage as much. He wanted to provide her with his strength, his know-how, and his abilities. Let her lean on him.

God, apparently, had other plans.

She ran her hands over the bandage, perhaps checking the firmness of the wrappings. "Did you hear about Jonas?"

Who had told her? Was there no end to the burdens she carried? Wyatt laid back. "Yes."

As for himself, he had not received the news well. But his heart was torn. How far could a man be pushed before falling off the precipice?

Katie's labor had only just begun before he stopped it, saving her and their baby. Still, it had ripped Wyatt to emotional shreds. What would he do if it happened again? If it couldn't be stopped and he lost her? And their child?

What if he'd trusted another doctor and that man couldn't save her? Wouldn't he be angry? Wouldn't he seek vengeance?

He would make certain that Jonas answered for his crimes. But in the midst of it all, Wyatt's heart hurt for the man's loss, and he knew he would be able to release this anger.

"And you lay here as if I told you he cheated at a horse race." Her face colored. Was she so angered?

Wyatt caught her hand and pulled her closer. "If you think I was not every bit as ready to exact my own brand of justice upon the man for what he did, you are wrong. I did want to hurt him. Badly."

Her eyes welled.

"But then I let my heart talk to my brain. He is a wayward soul, a marred soul. And he seeks something he cannot have—restitution. As if that will make what happened all right. Can you not see that?"

Katie sniffled. Her eyes glazed with moisture. Then her features twisted. "I am not so ready to absolve him." She turned, jerking her arm from him.

He did not release it. "Neither am I, Katie."

Her struggle to pull away halted, but she would not face him.

"Jonas will have his day with the judge. And he will answer for what he has done. But I refuse to become him in the process."

Katie's other hand pressed to her face.

"Please..." he spoke, his words soft. "Come here."

She turned, her face a mess of tears and wayward emotion. "I don't know what to feel. What to think."

He tugged at her hand once more.

She required no further encouragement to lay beside him.

As she settled, he gathered her in his arms.

He kissed the top of her head. "Let's ask God what He thinks."

Christmas was less than a week away. Katherine moved about

the clinic. But instead of medicinals, she sifted through boxes of decorations.

Wyatt managed to make it down the stairs. Though he still had the cane, it marked a big step forward in his recovery.

Katherine afforded him a nod and a smile. "Glad to see you up and about."

He nodded.

Pulling her hair over her shoulder, she dug into the crate on the exam table. Hadn't she seen that red ribbon in here? Perhaps it sank to the bottom.

"What's all this?" He waved a hand over the room.

"I'm behind in getting the final touches on the church." She continued to search, not taking even a moment to look at him.

"Katie." His voice was flat. Was he unsettled?

She glanced up at him. "Yes?"

He stared at her, his eyes widening.

She met his gaze, equally intense. What did he intend? Was she not managing as he expected?

"You don't mean that you still intend to decorate and make merry?" he said, a bit loudly and abrupt.

Her brows furrowed. He couldn't mean it. She had to finish the task set before her. So many people relied on her. And what would the holiday be without proper decor and organized festivities? "Of course. It's Christmas."

He stepped closer. "Christmas? I thought we agreed we didn't need all this," he said as he grabbed for a piece of garland from the nearest crate and held it up, "to celebrate. That we need only our family...together. A day of peace to recognize Christ come to earth."

Her gaze flitted over the boxes. Christmas wouldn't be the same without these things, would it? "But the town expects a church warm with green holly and red ribbon and—"

"I don't *care* what the town wants. The only thing I care about is your well-being." He was in her face now.

Heat stirred within her. "As you see, Dr. Sullivan." She clutched the crate, balancing it from underneath. "I am well enough."

Grabbing for the box, he returned it to the exam table. "Not well enough to carry these around Cripple Creek, hanging things here and there, and wearing yourself thin."

She hardened her gaze. "Are you telling me *not* to do this?"

Letting out a long breath, he said, "Katie, I think we are both on edge. Let's take a moment and think."

He was right. They should be like-minded and gracious with one another. She let her shoulders drop. "I agree. We *are* on the same team."

He nodded.

Locking eyes with him, she turned her lips upward just a bit. How could she make him understand? "I just...have so much going wrong lately, I need to bring some yuletide cheer into this town. It is what they asked me to do."

"That was before. No one will blame you if you put an end to all this and focus on your family. Sometimes, Katie," he said, shuffling his feet and looking at the floor. Then he caught her gaze again. "I get the feeling you are trying to escape."

"Escape?" Her hand flew to her chest. He couldn't mean that.

"You have pretty high-minded ideas about people and what they will think about you. So you shove your own problems to the side, sacrificing yourself for that laud."

Of all the...

"Wyatt Sullivan, you take that back." She bit at her lip.

His thinned.

"That was just the meanest..." Pushing the crate farther away, she turned and walked out the door. She couldn't take his hard words, or the reality of them, any longer.

How could these charred remains have been their home? The place where they became a family?

Wyatt stood in the space that was once between the barn and house, staring at the ruined shambles of memories.

But that wasn't true.

He still remembered...so clearly.

Yes, he saw in his mind's eye the evening they brought Jack and Susie home. To this house. And the days, the events that saw his and Katie's relationship grow from contained animosity, denied attraction in reality, to love. A love so deep and so real it opened a part of him he never knew could exist again. The part that had been dormant from the wounds inflicted from childhood.

He prayed the hardships of these last weeks would not likewise stunt Jack or Susie. Why couldn't he have protected them? That had been his promise. To himself. To Katie.

Looking toward the ground, he fought the voice that taunted, calling him a failure. Wouldn't he prefer to lean on God's truth? Wasn't that what he had come to learn? That he was, in fact, powerless on his own? His only hope was in God's plan and provision.

Footfalls behind him drew his attention from the disaster tearing at his heart.

He turned.

"The barn ain't been touched." Jack came up beside him.

Letting out a breath, Wyatt studied the structure behind him. He was thankful for that. The horses had been saved that night. And the efforts of the townsmen had been successful in sparing the barn.

But he couldn't keep Jack's gaze off the now unrecognizable house.

"What should we do, Pa? Is there's anything worth saving?"

Wyatt frowned. There may be something here or there. Perhaps. But nothing would have escaped either flame and water. Probably both.

He shook his head. "No. I don't. Sorry, son. I know you were hoping—"

Jack waved a hand. "It's all right."

Wyatt laid an arm on the boy's shoulders. Though Jack had not voiced it, he knew the youngster had a few things he kept from his childhood to remember his birth parents.

Why he felt he couldn't share that with Wyatt, he didn't know. But he would give Jack space to reveal it in his own time. Still, the loss of those things may very well bring on a grief for his parents that he had not quite known.

Jack sniffled.

Wyatt gripped his shoulder. "It's hard, I know."

The boy nodded.

"But we choose how we see this." Wyatt scanned the rubble once more.

He sensed Jack's eyes on him. Looking over, he met the boy's confused gaze.

"Life is full of endings. But it's also full of beginnings. We can choose to focus on this as an ending. Or think of it as a beginning."

Jack shifted his focus to the remains of the house. Was he considering Wyatt's words?

A stillness fell between them in that space. It was pleasant. Peaceful.

Jack broke it. "Kind of like an adventure."

Wyatt moved his hand to rub the back of the boy's neck. He would do what he could to keep their eyes turned toward the future. To focus on what would be, not what was. In order to do that, he must set his heart and feet to do so first.

The baby would be here soon. And he or she would usher in a fresh start of a new kind. Their family would change. Forever. Their roles would all change, if only a bit.

Wait...

Didn't Jack say the barn was untouched?

"Jack, there was no damage in the barn?" Wyatt looked at his son.

"No. I didn't see any."

Wyatt turned and walked, somewhat awkwardly to the large, red structure.

Jack caught up to him easily. "What is it, Pa?"

How could Wyatt have forgotten it? He made his way to the far corner, maneuvering past the stalls, around the mess, and to the old farming implements—the long-forgotten corner.

"What do you need with this stuff?" Jack stood beside him.

Wyatt glanced at him. And smiled. "I have a surprise."

The boy's forehead creased.

"But I think I'll need your help."

CHAPTER 8

Once Upon A Christmas

Katherine stared at the wooden cross, fixed on the back wall of the church. She couldn't help but cringe at the complete lack of decoration around her. Had she failed? Or had God failed her?

That didn't seem an entirely appropriate thing to think.

Was it acceptable to question God?

She stood from the pew she had taken refuge in about halfway down the aisle. Sliding into the walkway between the rows of benches, she let her senses take in the church, its serene and humble atmosphere.

The people who came week after week did not come because they lacked hope. No, they believed, they trusted in a God who could save them. Who cared about them. Didn't she?

She thought she did.

Believed she did.

But now...

Her steps took her to the altar. She ran her hand along its surface—smoothed with time and the many who had knelt there and beseeched the Lord.

Dare she?

Adjusting her skirts and her larger stomach, she dropped to her knees. And prayed.

About Wyatt, the house, her children, the baby...

But her thoughts drifted often and her prayer felt forced. Because God wasn't there? Or because she had been cut off from Him?

Letting out a breath, deeper than she'd had in a while, she sought not the cross, but her own heart. Her stance became not that of a folded-hands, straight-backed, pious seeker, but she hunched over the top of the altar.

Where did her heart lie?

She remained. How long, she did not know. Her knees ached and her back muscles spasmed.

Pushing up from the altar, she stood. Her whole body had become stiff. She stretched. That did not provide much relief to her back. Strange, it seemed her lower back hurt the most.

Lifting her eyes once more to the cross, she frowned. It seemed He would not move in her this day. Would not confirm His presence in her or in this place. Had it all been something she'd conjured?

She didn't wish to believe that. But, how did she get here —house gone, overstretched, overwhelmed, and ready to give up? If God loved her as He promised...how did she end up here?

Turning, she grimaced and put a hand to her lower back. How was it that the pain could intensify? She must have truly kinked something.

Taking in as much of a breath as she could and forcing it out, she relented.

If these were the tidings she received preceding a day of celebrating *His* Son's arrival, perhaps she shouldn't be so concerned after Christmas either. After all, hadn't she endured enough? And if the town wanted someone to care, they needed to find that person. Because she didn't. Not anymore.

She straightened her shoulders and took the steps that would remove her from this place.

Sharp pain flared through her lower back. It took her breath away. She grabbed the edge of a pew to keep upright.

Was something wrong with the baby? This didn't seem right.

Wyatt.

She had to get to Wyatt.

The pain struck again, forcing her to her knees as she cried out, her voice echoing in the empty building.

Why? Why had she come alone?

Her breaths came in heaves now. Sweat covered her face. Where was Wyatt? How could she find him?

A rush overcame her—something was about to happen. But what? There was a release, a rupture of some sort. And warm liquid ran down her legs. A lot of warm liquid.

What was it? Blood? Was she losing the baby?

Sensation flashed through her body. She trembled and shook. Her body had become weak. So weak. Could she make it to the door? Could she even stand?

Then another pain hit. More intense. Like fire.

Wyatt covered the precious, now completed cradle. It sat in the corner of Jack's makeshift bedroom above the clinic.

"Thanks for your help," he said to David. "Glad you were headed our way."

David's gaze remained on the gift, now indistinguishable under the blanket. Was something on his mind?

Their interchange had been somewhat strained when they crossed paths just moments ago on the main street. But Wyatt was sincere in his gratitude. Why did it seem David was none too happy about it?

But Wyatt wasn't so daft. This tension was because of Jonas.

Did David feel responsible in some way? Or did he think Wyatt blamed him?

"David?" Wyatt tried, shifting so he faced his brother-in-law.

The other man neither moved nor acknowledged Wyatt's entreaty.

Wyatt cleared his throat. "I think we need to get something in the open." He crossed his arms.

David sighed and dropped his head, now looking at the floor. "I've never been good at that kind of thing."

"Me neither." Wyatt let his gaze wander to the window. People milled about below, going about their lives. So fortunate.

David grunted.

"But your sister..." Wyatt turned his attention back to David, who raised his gaze at those words. "She has certainly worked hard to change that."

The man, who knew as well as he did about Katie's persuasive powers, smiled.

Wyatt lifted one side of his mouth. "Surely you know I wouldn't hold another's actions against you."

David nodded and looked to the window again. "I believe that."

What was this tension then? Why would David still act as if a gulf separated them?

Wyatt opened his mouth, but David spoke before he could.

"What of my own actions?" David's gaze bore into Wyatt.

There was a moment of confusion, but it was fleeting.

Wyatt wished it hadn't been. Did he keep a record of wrongs? Against Katie's family?

David referred to their heated conversation that evening after Katie went into labor. Wyatt remembered David's insinuations, even outright accusations all too well.

He longed to speak of it all being forgiven. But was it? The quickness of the wrong coming to memory was not a good sign.

Wyatt swallowed. And continued to search for words both helpful and true.

"I had no right." David's voice shook, yet only just.

How difficult was it for David to keep himself together? Wyatt, too, struggled.

Biting his lip, Wyatt nodded.

David looked to the toe of his boot as he shuffled his feet.

Would this thing between them remain? Could they return to the comfortable camaraderie they'd had? How?

"Let's make a deal, you and I." Wyatt took a step forward.

David peered at Wyatt, one eyebrow up. Was he so skeptical?

"You don't expect me to be perfect. And I won't expect you to be."

Both of David's brows rose. Was that interest?

"We won't judge each other for not measuring up." Wyatt unfolded his arms. "We'll just be who we are and let that be that."

David's gaze held Wyatt's. Was he thinking? Or did he not care to repair what had been lost?

Wyatt stuck out his hand.

It only took five seconds for David to take it.

All Katherine knew was this burning pain. She shut her eyes against it, but that did nothing to abate the sheer magnitude of it.

She sat on the floor now, on her right hip, struggling with every breath to simply pull air in and push it out.

Would anyone come? Or would she and her baby die here?

The pain intensified again. It originated in her abdomen now, but filled her whole being.

She screamed. As much to be heard as for the pain. But the church was set back, a bit away from town. Her only hope was that the pastor would return from his noon meal.

Please, do. And soon!

Where was Wyatt? Was he worried about her? She shouldn't have stormed out of the clinic like she had this morning. He only wished to help her. And she had dismissed him and his words.

She had gained nothing for it. Nothing but pain.

Crying out again, she released herself to lay on the dirt-ridden floorboards. That was the least of her concerns.

The pain was so great. It would surely tear her apart. If only she could see Wyatt one more time...

Hinges squealed.

The door?

It must be her hopeful imaginings. Everything seemed hazy.

"Hello?" a deep voice called from the direction of the entrance.

She croaked out something, uncertain it made sense.

Footsteps, heavy, landed on the wooden floor.

"Mrs. Sullivan!"

A thud. Was something dropped? If only she could see through this cloud. Or sense anything through the pain.

She cried out as another wave ripped through her body.

"Lord help you, ma'am, that baby is comin'!" The voice was now above her. The masculine presence so near.

Lifting her head but the tiniest bit, she saw a dark-skinned man. She knew him.

Mr. Jeffries!

But how had he found her?

His hands hovered over her body. "I don't know what to do. You need the doctor."

"Please..." she managed.

"I'm afraid to move you. But I'm afraid to leave you." She could almost feel the man's panic.

Reaching for his hand, she squeezed it. Even she sensed it was a weak effort. "We go."

He nodded. "All right."

Arms moved under her, shifting her body.

She yelped.

"I'm awful sorry, ma'am."

She shook her head. "We go."

Once he lifted her, relief filled her.

There was hope.

Wyatt and David stepped out of the clinic.

"Katie and Mary sure have done a fine job of decorating the main square." David tipped his head toward the large tree.

Wyatt nodded, but didn't have anything to add. He was none too pleased with the whole thing. For it had cost Katie dearly. Had cost *them* dearly.

Still, it meant something to Katie. Should he have given that more consideration? Had he been too dismissive? Perhaps he should have another conversation with her about it.

"Doc!" a boy ran down the main road, headed straight for

them. "Doc!" He came closer, stopping just short of where Wyatt and David stood.

"Slow down there." Wyatt held out his hands. "What's the matter?"

"That large, dark man is bringing your wife. She's dead," the boy declared and turned as if he would run off.

Wyatt's heart stopped.

David caught the boy before he escaped. "Dead? What do you mean 'dead'?"

"She ain't movin' and he's got an awful mean look on his face." The youngster scowled.

Wyatt grabbed a handful of David's shirt at his shoulder as the large figure appeared at the edge of the street. Indeed he did carry Katie. And she wasn't moving. She hung from the man's outstretched arms. Lifeless. Was she?

Wyatt couldn't bring in enough air all of a sudden.

David gripped his arm.

Would he have fallen if not for the support?

"We don't know anything yet," David said. Though he stood next to Wyatt, he seemed far away.

Wyatt wasn't sure he could remain upright. But...

If she wasn't dead.

If she needed him.

He had to be strong. Put on the doctor.

For her.

Taking in a ragged breath, he stood straighter and let the physician slide into place.

The dark-skinned man approached rapidly. And as he drew nearer, Wyatt became more and more uneasy about Katie's limp form.

No.

He must do this. For her.

If he had to repeat that every minute, he would.

The large man was close enough that Wyatt saw the rise and fall of Katie's chest.

Praise God!

He had never been so thankful.

As much as he wished to take her from the man and cradle her in his arms, he needed her on the exam table. So instead, he opened the door and ushered the man inside.

"I found her in the church, doctor. In a bad way." The man laid her on the exam table.

Wyatt nodded. The words turned his stomach, but he remembered…he was the doctor now. For her.

"I was walking by after delivering some firewood to the church and heard her." The man stepped back and slid his hat off as Wyatt stumbled around Katie's still form.

Oh, this leg.

Wyatt met the man's eyes. "I thank you, sir. But I'm afraid I have to ask you to step out."

The man nodded. "Can I do anything?"

"The Widow Johnson. Can you get her?" Wyatt stepped to his cabinet and grabbed out several utensils. Many he hoped he wouldn't have to use.

"Yes, sir. Right away." The man moved out of the clinic, shutting the door behind himself.

Wyatt glanced at his wife, unconscious. How long had she been in pain, and all alone, before she passed out?

David barged through the door. "Did you just ask that man to bring Widow Johnson here?"

Wyatt turned his back to David, his focus on his medicinals. "Yes, I did."

"Timothy's mother? As in, Timothy—the man who felt you betrayed him? The man who wanted to marry my sister? Who had to leave town because of you two?"

"The same one." Wyatt closed the cabinet, certain he had pulled out everything he might need.

"Why?"

Wyatt shot him a look. "No one will reach Dr. Brown in time. I may have to do surgery and I'll need help. Widow Johnson has been this town's midwife since before I was born."

"Do you trust her?" David said, exasperation in his voice. "You don't think she might harbor resentment for you two? For Katie?"

Wyatt's gaze fixed on his beloved. "I have to take that chance."

For her.

K atherine wasn't certain which was worse—the darkness or the struggle against it. Something drew her to fight it, but she wasn't sure what it was.

How was she even aware she was in darkness? What manner of dream was this? Wasn't it only when awaking that she determined she had slept? How, then, was she so aware of her own sleep now?

Or was this not sleep? But something else?

She pulled out of the thick darkness, jerking the tendrils of her thoughts free of it until nothing held her.

Crying. Someone cried.

For her?

Was she needed?

Her body told her it was so. A part of her ached for the tiny cry.

Mustering all her courage and energy, she gave one great push off from the nothingness.

And opened her eyes.

She lay in her and Wyatt's bed in the clinic.

And there was pain. But it was more ache than the sharp pain she had known.

The cry was louder. Much louder.

A baby.

Her hand found her abdomen.

Though not completely flat, it was not round either.

Was the cry from her baby?

She pushed up with her arms. The ache became more deeply sore in her belly and she clenched her teeth against it.

"Wyatt?" She wished for him as much as she asked.

A shifting beside her alerted her that she was not alone.

Turning her head, she saw that Wyatt straightened himself in a chair. Had he fallen asleep watching over her?

"Wyatt!" She reached for him.

He caught her hand as he scooted the chair closer to the bed. "Yes, Katie darling?" His eyes shone bright.

Tears filled hers. "Am I...?"

He searched her face.

"Are we...?"

His fingers grazed the side of her face. "You are well, my love. We are well."

"Our baby?" Her words were more mouthed than actually spoken.

He smiled. "Yes. Let me introduce you." Turning toward the door, he called, "Aunt Mary!"

Mary? What part did she play in all of this?

Soon enough, but not as quickly as Katherine would have liked, Mary stepped through the door carrying a fussing bundle.

"I am so glad you are awake. As is this one. Someone's hungry." Mary smiled and handed the baby to Wyatt.

Katherine sat straighter. Was that squirming little thing her baby? He or she seemed so small. So helpless.

But the babe was no doubt hungry. How was she

supposed to prepare to feed her baby? She'd never done so. Did she—?

"I would like you to meet...our daughter." Wyatt held the little one at an angle so Katherine could see her face.

Her heart melted. As did her emotions. They poured out without any effort to stop them.

Wyatt sat on the bed next to Katherine.

She was captivated by her daughter, still crying. Someone would have to show her how to nourish the baby. And soon.

"I hope you don't mind." Wyatt looked at her.

Tearing her eyes from the child, who bore Katherine's red-brown hair and Wyatt's blue eyes, she caught his gaze.

"But I think she and I have settled on a name."

"Oh?" Katherine furrowed her eyebrows. Why would Wyatt—?

"Ellie Mae."

Katherine's breath caught. Her childhood best friend. The friend who's untimely death had affected her friendship with Wyatt, but also sealed their fate. "It's perfect."

"I think we should get her eating." Wyatt maneuvered the small girl into Katherine's arms.

She was so light. But Katherine's heart became full, and so heavy.

"How do I do this?" Glancing up at Mary, Katherine found that her sister-in-law had vanished. So she turned to her husband. "Help me?"

"Of course."

It took some work on both their parts, but Ellie Mae was nursing within several minutes.

"So..." Katherine leaned her head on her husband's shoulder. "Did you need Dr. Brown after all?"

"Yes," Wyatt said simply.

"Oh?" Why couldn't Wyatt deliver her? And where was Dr. Brown?

"But we would never have reached him in time." Wyatt ran a hand along her arm.

What, then, did he mean? Had he delivered her alone? Or with help? Did Mary help?

"Widow Johnson assisted." Wyatt turned and spoke into her hair. "Or maybe I should say I assisted her."

"Widow Johnson? Timothy's mother?" Had he taken such measures?

"Yes. I didn't trust myself to be at my best with my injury. And you needed the best I could offer. In this case, that wasn't me."

"Hmmm." It would take more than a moment for her to think through the events of the last day.

And pretty soon all would be upended again when they would introduce Jack and Susie to their new sister.

But for now, she found peace in what was. She was well. Wyatt was here. And Ellie Mae had arrived.

The climb up and down the clinic stairs had become second nature. Did Wyatt even need the cane anymore? Or did he use it to make himself feel better?

This was, indeed, a Christmas to remember.

But was it?

He paused to think on that, remembering how he had rejected Katherine's desires for holiday festivities and merriment.

Had he even cared to discover just why it was so important for her?

No. His own concerns had been foremost in his mind. Perhaps he wasn't wrong for that—her well-being had been his first priority.

But perhaps he should give a thought to her desires.

Was it too late?

What was it that made this holiday important to her?

A plan began to form in his mind.

Could he pull it off?

If everyone pitched in—and that meant *everyone*—they just might be able to.

Where was Mary?

Would Katherine ever tire of admiring her daughter? She didn't think so. Ellie Mae was so perfect. Her little nose, and tiny lips, and sweet fingers. How could so much love be in one person? And as much as Katherine loved this little bundle, it did not diminish her love for Susie or Jack.

Wyatt had brought them in to meet their sister yesterday. Jack already adored the baby girl. Susie was much more interested in what Santa might bring her.

Katherine's heart sank. What could she do about that? Nothing from her recovery bed. And she doubted Wyatt would see to it. He was a regular old Scrooge these days.

But they would all be together. No matter what.

She glanced out the window. Dusk had settled over the town and the streets had cleared. Where had everyone gone?

And Wyatt? Was he putting Susie to bed?

Laying down, she stilled her mind. It wouldn't be long before Ellie Mae needed to nurse. Glancing at the babe once more in her makeshift bed nearby brought Katherine such sweet peace. She closed her eyes.

An angel chorus sang in the heavens above her.

What?

That couldn't be.

She opened her eyes, lifting her head and shoulders off the bed.

It was there—the chorus of voices. What were they singing? And where did the sound come from?

As she listened, the words became clearer.

"What child is this, who lay to rest on Mary's lap, is sleeping? Whom angels..."

The singing continued and became louder. Katherine sat up in the bed and peered at the window. It was closed, but the curtains were open. She caught a glimmer of candlelight. What was that?

A crowd of townsfolk came into view on the main street below. They approached slowly, each bearing a candle as they sang her favorite Christmas song.

They broke into the chorus, and the door to her room opened.

Wyatt, Jack, and Susie entered. Her husband and son held small candles and they joined the voices below. "This, this, is Christ the King, whom shepherds guard and angels sing. Haste, haste, to bring Him laud, the babe, the son of Mary."

Her heart swelled and her eyes filled. Who had arranged this? Could it have been Wyatt? Why? For her?

Jack sat his and Wyatt's candles on the side table and grabbed up Susie.

Wyatt helped Katherine to a chair, already set by the window. He wrapped a blanket around her shoulders and opened the small, glass panes.

The main square was lovely. How had she not noticed it had been finished and fully decorated?

As the carol came to an end, the townsfolk surrounded the tree and sang *Silent Night*.

Katherine couldn't contain her tears. She reached for Wyatt and took his hand. Looking up, she met his gaze. "Thank you. So much."

He smiled. "That's not all."

As that song ended, the door opened again. David entered carrying a large object covered in a blanket.

She glanced at Wyatt. What had he done?

Setting the oversized bundle in front of her, David put a hand to her shoulder and kissed the side of her face. "Merry Christmas, Katie. Your husband wanted it to be special."

She grabbed her brother's hand with her free one. "Merry Christmas."

He slipped free and stepped away.

"Go ahead." Wyatt waved at the covered object. "Open it."

"Oh, Wyatt." She fingered the blanket. "I...I didn't get you anything."

"Nonsense." He leaned closer. "You gave me the best gift I could ask for." His gaze flickered to the sleeping Ellie Mae.

She smiled. Turning back to the blanket, she pulled it from her Christmas present.

And gasped.

How did he know? It was the very thing she wanted most. The thing they now needed more than anything else—a cradle for Ellie Mae. And she knew somehow without asking that it had been hewn by her husband's hands.

She clapped her hand over her heart. Would it burst from her chest?

"It was a labor of love," Wyatt whispered, now closer to her ear. "And Jack helped with the final touches."

Turning to Wyatt, already so close, she lifted her hands and framed his face. And brought his lips to hers.

As the crowd below broke out in a robust rendition of *We Wish You A Merry Christmas*, she knew there would never be a happier Christmas.

God had heard her prayer. He *had* been with her. All along. Just as He promised. Emmanuel.

Epilogue

One Year Later

Katherine watched Ellie Mae crawl toward her brother. Could the small girl truly be a year old? It didn't seem possible, but the year had passed slowly all the same.

The year had been difficult, but they were in the house now. And well settled. Wyatt had poured every available moment into rebuilding. Their home was beautiful. Everything she could have hoped for.

Wyatt picked up Ellie Mae and wrapped an arm around Jack.

The boy had shot up in the last couple of months. Would he ever stop growing? His interest in reading mysteries deepened and he had begun regaling his family with his own stories.

But Susie had perhaps changed the most—talking and even starting to read. But she seemed less baby now, more little girl. Her hair had grown in length and thickness. Now her curls slid down her back, giving Katherine a lot of trouble when it came time to brush it. And she was the best little helper with her sister.

As Wyatt stepped across the room, Katherine wondered if anyone would notice his slight limp. Unless they were looking for it. He sat by Katherine and gave her a wink. "The tree is lovely."

This year, Katherine had focused on their own celebration, letting responsibility for the town's festivities fall to someone else. It was worth it.

Their family tree, decorated with ribbon and popcorn, provided an added warmth to the great room. It had become a wonderful draw for them as they gathered around it each evening. And that's all she wanted—family togetherness as they worshipped God and remembered the birth of His Son.

Wyatt's deep baritone hummed a tune.

Ellie Mae leaned against his chest.

Katherine closed her eyes and let the melody fill her.

Soon enough, he vocalized the words to *O Holy Night* as Katherine pulled Susie into her lap, hugging the child and pressing a kiss to her head.

And it was...a most holy night indeed.

The train jerked as it slowed and stopped. But the passenger paid it no mind. He was home. For how long, he did not know. Had time healed old wounds? Or would his heart ache as if the slighting had happened recently?

Gathering his few things, he joined the small crowd moving toward the exit.

He peered through a window in an attempt to spy his mother. Her last letter said she would come. Would she? Or would the cold keep her in?

It was no matter.

Stepping down onto the platform, he turned this way and that, taking in the sights and atmosphere of Cripple Creek.

Regardless of the train and other changes, it was home. And always would be. How could he have let *her* run him off? No longer.

And so, he squared his shoulders, all the more determined to go after his mission.

Yes, whether or not this town was ready, whether *she* was ready, Timothy Johnson had arrived.

Keep reading for a preview of the next book in the Cripple Creek Series!

Thank you, dear reader, for for reading along with me! If you enjoyed this story, I would sincerely appreciate if you would submit a review. It would mean so much to me!

To read more about these characters, follow along with the Cripple Creek Series. Find it at:
https://saraturnquist.com/cripple-creek-series/

It has been such fun to revisit the fictional people in Cripple Creek, Colorado (which is, of course, a real town). We have seen how Wyatt and Katherine are getting along and how the town is faring.

This has been a one-shot Christmas novella that has sparked my interest to expand *Hope in Cripple Creek* into a series! So, look for more books on the horizon.

Much of what you read is absolutely fictional in all accounts. The details about the railroad coming were based in research and the fire hints at a great fire that came upon Cripple Creek devastated the whole town, but not until April 29, 1869, whereas this novella is set in the winter.

And then, of course, in the Epilogue we see the return of Timothy (from the first book) to Cripple Creek. What will this mean for Katherine and Wyatt? Why is Timothy back? I can't wait to find out!

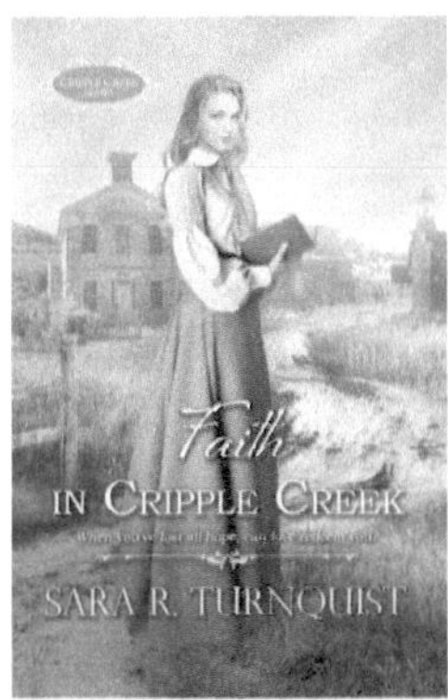

This had to be the worst day of her life. Jane Millington opened her eyes. Had the stagecoach stopped? Her teeth still seemed to vibrate despite the lack of forward momentum.

Indeed, her eyes confirmed what her body could not—the shaking heat box on wheels no longer sped through the town.

She looked out the window and coughed. Dust surrounded the vehicle. Still, she peered beyond. The stores, rustic to be sure, lined the main stretch. Did everything have to be covered in dirt? The buildings looked as if a thorough scrub would do them good. But what could she expect from such a provincial town?

Her gaze wandered to the platform. The small cluster of people looking in the direction of the coach did not seem threatening. But where was her friend? She had endured this journey with only that hope intact—that she would see Kitty, her dearest, closest friend at its conclusion.

"Miss?" a rough voice cut through the fog surrounding her thoughts.

The driver stood beneath the door, a worn expression on his face. For certain, the trip jarred him as much as it had her. Why, then, did he insist on traveling at such speeds?

"We're here," he continued.

As she watched, limbs still frozen in place, he reached for the latch and opened the door.

"Cripple Creek." He spat. Something dark and foul came from his mouth, landing a short distance from him in the dirt.

Jane swallowed and her stomach twisted. Was such a lack of manners common in Cripple Creek?

"You all right, miss?" The driver looked at her again, an eyebrow raised.

How could she tell him about the roiling in her stomach? Which was more to blame—the upset of the coach ride or the small dark wet puddle inches from the man's boot?

"You seem a bit...pale." The driver's features shifted from the stale tired expression to one that mimicked concern.

"I'm..." She wanted to say *quite well*. But her inability to quell her nausea did not help matters. She peeled her fingers loose from the window opening and pressed the back of her hand to her lips. Perhaps that would prevent an unladylike and untimely emptying of her last meal.

"I don't need this," the man declared. He turned away, muttering something about 'females.'

Her face heated. Not a pleasant addition to her unease.

"Sir," the driver called to someone farther away. "I got a lady needs a doctor. You know where I can find one?"

Jane shut her eyes. This wasn't happening.

"Miss?" another, somewhat kinder voice spoke into the confining space.

She only dared open one eye to see who else had come to witness her embarrassment. Oh, why hadn't someone been sent to meet her? Kitty had *promised* that she would be here.

The man that now looked in seemed genuine in his concern. He was taller than the driver. Broader of shoulder. His dark hair grew past his collar, and his unshaven face betrayed the beginnings of a beard. But it was his eyes…his deep brown eyes, mirrors of her own…that caught her. When she met his gaze, she could breathe again.

"May I take you to the town's doctor?" His voice was smooth even as his eyes seemed pained. By what?

"I…I…" This was not the time to lose her words! She sucked in a breath and let it out slowly. "I think I may just need some fresh air." Indeed her uneasiness abated now that the coach had stilled.

The man with the brown eyes turned his head. What did he seek?

No one stood behind him.

The driver had moved off. Where had he gone? Surely, he wouldn't abandon his responsibility.

Her would-be savior shot out a breath. "Typical."

What did that mean?

He turned back to her. "Please, miss, let me help you." Extending his hand into the coach, he waited.

And waited.

His gaze landed on her, a question in his eyes.

Was she staring? She jerked back. And almost toppled off the bench.

Hands gripped her forearms.

As she righted herself, she found she was only inches from the man. Had he stepped into the coach?

She couldn't tear her eyes away from his enough to take in the situation. As she blinked, she became more aware of their precarious positioning. And her cheeks warmed once again.

"Are you sure you don't need to see the doctor?" His eyes darkened. He did seem rather concerned.

"No, sir. I thank you. But I am quite well." Though she asserted it to be so, her voice sounded weak even to her.

He pulled back, stepping out of the coach. But he kept a firm hold on one of her hands. And so, as he removed himself from the space, he brought her as well.

Now in the open, she blinked against the bright sunlight. And allowed him to guide her forward as her eyes adjusted.

She took in her surroundings once again. She had a better view of the rows of buildings lining the main dirt road. It was more than she'd expected of this small town. Still not what she would consider a comfortable place to live by any means. How did one survive with so few businesses to patronize? But it was quaint. Endearing even. Though perhaps impossible to clean.

"Is someone expecting you?"

The man's question drew her attention back to his face. With his mouth drawn into a thin line and his brows furrowed, she wouldn't say he welcomed her interrupting his day.

Pity.

She looked away, chastising herself for thinking such a thing. That wasn't right. It wasn't as if she were free to notice such things.

"Miss?" His head dipped and he squeezed her hand.

Only then did she realize he still held to her fingers. His touch anchored her and sent tingles up her arm. Goodness, she was out of sorts.

"I...did expect my friend to meet me. She must have been delayed."

He frowned as he glanced down the street. As if seeking out some sort of salvation.

How did she get herself into such messes?

Sighing, he released her hand. Did he just now realize he retained his hold? "I can't very well leave you standing out here. Alone."

"That's kind of you, sir. But I can manage until..."

He waved a hand between them. "Let me walk you to the café. At least there you'll be comfortable while you wait."

She swallowed. Should she take him up on his offer? Or dismiss his aid? He appeared rather put off already. But maybe that was just her own embarrassment. There was no reason to think him anything other than a perfect gentleman.

"Thank you," was all she managed.

He nodded. "I suppose it's the least I can do."

As he turned, she wondered after his statement. He had already assisted her rather awkward exit from the coach.

The coach!

She put a hand on his forearm. "My bags—"

He turned only halfway. "The driver will put them by the telegraph office. They'll be safe there."

Uncertain, she glanced at the small building beside the stagecoach where the driver piled bags and trunks.

When she shifted her focus back to her guide, he stared at her hand upon his arm.

She snapped it back as quickly as possible.

His eyes found hers once more. There was something deeper in those hazelnut orbs than she could discern. Something swirling in his thoughts. It entranced her.

"Please," he said as he held out a hand toward the far end of the road. "Shall we continue?"

"Yes." She picked up step beside him.

The silence between them became tense. She so dreaded silence, and the awkwardness that came with it.

"I'm Jane," she spit out.

"Miss?"

"My name—Jane Millington." She allowed herself another glance in his direction.

He was not looking at her. Rather his face turned opposite, peering at something in the distance.

Her introduction and his lack of response did nothing to improve the awkwardness. Perhaps it even made it worse.

He veered to the right and stopped just short of an open door. There were tables and chairs within and the smell of meat and vegetables. As well as cobbler.

Her stomach growled. It had been a while since she'd eaten. But she wasn't certain if the gentleman would join her. Or was this where they parted?

Turning back to him, she pressed a smile to her lips. "I thank you... for your assistance."

He continued to watch the café. Was there something of great interest within? If so, she could not discern it.

Tightening her smile, she nodded and stepped over the threshold and into the café.

"Timothy."

She spun. "Pardon?"

"My name is Timothy. Perhaps I'll see you around town."

Her mouth moved, but no words came forth. And in the next instant, he had walked away.

She would have to ask about this Timothy. What, if anything, did her dear friend Katherine Matthews Sullivan know of him?

To read more, find *Faith in Cripple Creek* here:

https://saraturnquist.com/faith-in-cripple-creek/

Love in Cripple Creek (Book 4)

A woman burned by love. A man who has lost his way.

Betsy Callaway hasn't been the most upstanding person in Cripple Creek...and she has now passed the acceptable age for marriage. But something about her calls to Nikolai "Nick" Hammond's heart and draws him back home.

The antics that ensue between the pair and the obstacles they face--including their own stubbornness and becoming entangled in a bank robbery-- threaten to keep them on separate paths, but their draw to each other pushes them together.

Will the prodigal find home welcoming?
Can Betsy hope for real redemption?

And the prequels...

Lauren Crawford is nothing she should be. Put off by the War between the States and her own experience on her father's plantation, she longs for something more. Under the control of her parents, there is not much room for anything but submission. Still, she dares to defy them...

The war changed Tom Matthews. And he has plans of going beyond his father's humble farm. He will do whatever it takes to make those dreams come true. Until he finds himself drawn to a southern belle he would rather despise. He is soon caught up in a situation not of his own making.

How much is too much for the one he loves?
Dare he sacrifice his dream?

In the rugged terrains of Cripple Creek, David Matthews' world has always been overshadowed by his father. Each sunrise over Stoneybrook Ranch reminds him of the path laid out before him—a life scripted by expectations he isn't sure he can live up to.

Mary Foster has held a silent affection for David since their youth. And while her mother suffers the ravages of a disease they fight to contain, Mary's heart patiently beats in the hope that when David finds his place in the world, there might be room in it for her.

Will their paths diverge in the vast expanse of the frontier?
Or perhaps love can guide them to find in each other the very thing they are lacking in themselves—home.

Acknowledgments

There are many reasons I love writing and more specifically writing in this genre (clean Historical Romance). The people who have made this book possible are definitely a big part of that! And, once again, it is quite impossible to thank every person who touched this manuscript or my life in a significant way, but I will attempt to highlight those who were most prominent in this particular work.

To my beta reader, Mary Wood...you are amazing and you keep me turning in chapters. Thanks for kicking my butt.

For my editors, you keep me honest and have helped hone my words and make my work shine!

Cora Graphics, this cover art is amazing!

To Stephanie Taylor and Clean Reads...I am forever grateful for the support. And for believing in me. You are amazing.

To Word Weavers Page 13, I am so blessed to be with you, learning from you, and in fellowship with you all. Thanks for pointing out my weak areas with love and encouraging the strengths.

For Clarksville Christian Writers, y'all are my people.

Hannah R. Conway, I couldn't ask for a better writing mentor. You sharpen and spur me on in so many ways.

For my husband and kids, you keep me on my toes. In a good way!

For my dad, sister, and brother—this year was hard, but we held together. She would be proud. I know she would.

For my readers, thank you for gifting me with your time. You bless me so much.

About the Author

Sara is a coffee lovin', word slinging, Historical Romance author whose super power is converting caffeine into novels. She loves those odd little tidbits of history that are stranger than fiction. That's what inspires her. Well, that and a good love story.

But of all the love stories she knows, hers is her favorite. She lives happily with her own Prince Charming and their gaggle of minions. Three to be exact. They sure know how to distract a writer! But, alas, the stories must be written, even if it must happen in the wee hours of the morning.

Sara is an avid reader and enjoys reading and writing clean Historical Romance when she's not traveling.

Please follow along with her journey through her newsletter at: http://saraturnquist.com/list

Happy Reading!

facebook.com/AuthorSaraRTurnquist

instagram.com/sararturnquist

x.com/sararturnquist

youtube.com/@SaraRTurnquist

pinterest.com/sararturnquist

Also by
Sara R. Turnquist

CONVENIENT RISK SERIES

A Convenient Risk

An Inconvenient Christmas

A Less Convenient Path

A Convenient Escape

An Inconvenient Acquaintance

These Golden Years

A Less Convenient Arrangement

Ranch Hands Collection (ebook only)

LADY OF BOHEMIA SERIES

The Lady Bornekova

The Lady and the Hussites

The Lady and Her Champion

The Lady and Her Secret

RAILWAY ROMANCE SERIES

Laura, The Tycoon's Daughter

ACROSS THE YEARS SERIES

Among the Pages

Between the Lines

STANDALONE NOVELS

The General's Wife

Trail of Fears
Off to War

www.ingramcontent.com/pod-product-compliance
Lightning Source LLC
Chambersburg PA
CBHW021717190726
48289CB00008B/2578